THE FERRET

D1259086

TOM MINDER

Black Rose Writing | Texas

ISBN: 978-1-68433-659-3
PUBLISHED BY BLACK ROSE WRITING
www.blackrosewriting.com

Printed in the United States of America
Suggested Retail Price (SRP) $16.95

The Ferret is printed in Georgia

*As a planet-friendly publisher, Black Rose Writing does its best to eliminate unnecessary waste to reduce paper usage and energy costs, while never compromising the reading experience. As a result, the final word count vs. page count may not meet common expectations.

I would like to thank my editor Jim Davis from TypeRight Editing, and my beta readers Mark Doenges and Cassandra Ulrich from The South Jersey Writers' Group, Declan from Writerful Books, and Amanda Nicoler. Their feedback was helpful in tightening and smoothing out the plot.

I also appreciate the mentorship and comradery provided by The South Jersey Writers' Group and The Writers' Coffeehouse. Their feedback and constant encouragement helped to move this book forward.

THE FERRET

PART 1
TESTIMONY ACRES

CHAPTER 1

Salt Lake City

The father, mother, and five children stood on the hillcrest and marveled at the Great Salt Lake Valley below, their 1300 mile trek from Illinois completed. This was now home.

Louie studied the painting. *Such brave men and women. Seeking religious freedom, fighting off Spotted Fever, accepting their destiny. If only I could be so brave.* He pulled his smartphone. Finding Candy Crush Saga, he resumed his personal quest. Hard candies filled the screen as music chimed in arcade rhythm. He hummed and swiped with a purpose, removing obstacles, and hoping to dispose of the cherries blocking his path to level 636.

"Elder Kimball, I ask you to please maintain the sanctity of the Church Office Building. Guests pass through, and we want to project a focused respect for our mission," said Miriam, the office administrator. He closed the game, decided not to check Instagram, and slid the Droid into his Dockers.

He walked to a table lined with bottled water, juices, and periodicals. Filling a glass with Orangina, he picked up the latest issue of the Latter-Day Saints journal *Meridian* and returned to the overstuffed sofa. Setting the drink on a coaster (Miriam was watching), he looked over the room: high ceiling, oak molding, brass fixtures, a chandelier spreading light to every corner.

He found the index: Church, Society, Family, plenty of missionary stories, and the occasional cartoon. In the Sports section, he searched for news on BYU. *Not much here. Crap. They have a decent football team. How come no game action? At least a cheerleader or two would be nice to see.*

Bishop Warren emerged from his office, followed by men laughing at some remark uttered by the tall, thin, well-dressed man. Warren shook their hands and motioned to the door where a young man in a blue blazer stood. "Gentlemen, thanks for coming. Enjoy your time in Temple Square. David will show you around."

Warren winked at Louie. "Elder Kimball, please join me." He turned to Miriam. "Make sure we're not disturbed for the next 30 minutes."

The corner office was painted in a muted blue. Artwork depicting the 1847 trek to Utah hung on the wall. The floor-to-ceiling windows behind Warren's desk provided a panorama of the plaza: tourists, and men and women in white hurrying to their next destination. The bishop pointed to a leather-padded chair framed in oak.

Louie sat. On contact, the seat emitted a muffled sound that resembled a gastric condition. Warren laughed loud enough to make Miriam crane her neck. "I love that chair. Really loosens up a room."

Warren swiveled. "Now, Kimball. We've had our eyes on you. You're young, barely out of seminary, but know your trade, seem to have a nose for business, and, I hope, can keep a confidence. We need someone like you to head up construction for our southern Nevada real estate venture."

He picked up a remote, pointed to the far wall, and clicked. A screen descended, and a presentation opened, showing a vast stretch of barren desert. "This is the future site of Testimony Acres, a gated community of high-end homes, fifty miles north of Vegas." Next click. Women in the pool, their bathing suits providing minimal covering from the Nevada sun. "This will be a discrete vacation destination, Kimball. People need to relax and enjoy both privacy and the rugged surroundings."

Warren opened a drawer and took out a pamphlet, sliding it across the desk. "The men just in here are outside investors. Not Latter-day Saints, but distant cousins, if you will, The Community of Christ. They have deep pockets, and money to spend with little fanfare."

Next click. The Las Vegas skyline. "Reachable by a two-lane highway that the fine state of Nevada will soon upgrade to four. We're meeting with state officials now to help push this through their legislature. Fortunately, we have brothers and sisters in positions of influence. They'll convince doubters that the improvement will pay for itself over time."

Next click. "PRAISE BE TO GOD." Violet lettering on a background of the Mojave Desert. "There you have it. And you're in on the ground floor. You'll make sure the job is done, the money wisely spent, both on construction and human capital, and that the input from the non-LDS brethren is discrete."

He pulled a card from his pocket and placed it in front of Louie. "This is Leader Bradshaw. He'll be overseeing the project. He's in 316 upstairs and is awaiting your visit so we can kick this off."

He stood. "Good luck, Kimball. This will be quite lucrative for the LDS and participants such as yourself. God wants us to thrive and be wealthy. Let's not disappoint The Almighty."

"I won't let you down, Bishop Warren," he said taking the card. "Thanks for this opportunity."

Warren walked Louie to the door, slapped him on the shoulder, and sent him on his way.

Louie started for the elevator in the cavernous, echoing hallway. He beamed as Bishop Warren said to Miriam, "Nice young man, that Kimball."

"I guess so, Bishop Warren," she replied. "I wish he didn't look so much like a ferret."

Louie flinched at this, but walked on.

CHAPTER 2

Marty Bradshaw sat in his office, scrolling through his laptop and chuckling. He glanced up. Louie stood in the doorway.

"Hello, Leader Bradshaw. I'm Elder Kimball."

"Ah, you go by Louie, I hear. You come highly recommended by Bishop Warren." He gestured to a chair. "Take a load off. I was just checking Facebook." He closed the laptop. "I have to admit I love cat pictures. Those little goofballs."

Louie bent down to sit, feeling the leather before committing.

"Hah, It's OK, Louie. Warren's the practical joker. The chair is safe."

Louie made an act of faith and settled into the cushioned seat. He studied the arms and back, which were hewn into a likeness of a mountain lion, crouching and ready to attack prey.

"Isn't that neat?" Bradshaw asked. "Examine the legs. Wolves sitting, waiting for the cat to pounce. They'll be happy to pick over the leftovers."

Bradshaw turned toward the window. "It's a world of predator and prey, Louie. We must tame the earth until the Second Coming. Woe to the meek."

Louie pulled a small pad and pen from his shirt pocket. "So, Leader Bradshaw, Bishop Warren told me about Testimony Acres. Sounds like a big undertaking."

"No need for notes, Louie. We're going on a road trip to the Nevada desert so I can show you firsthand. Nothing like a long drive on a hundred-degree day to invigorate the spirit." He opened a drawer and removed a plastic bottle. "Here's some SPF 80. Best to put that on before we go out."

As Louie slathered, Bradshaw leaned over, continuing to search through his enormous desk. "Ah, here we go," he said, resurfacing. "He twirled a sky blue baseball cap. The front read Testimony Acres, the "o" replaced by the image of a blazing sun.

He tossed it to Louie, donned another for himself, and stood. "Let's do this, young man." He almost skipped to the door. "Besides, if we wait any longer, it will be a hundred-ten by the time we get there."

• • • • •

Bradshaw took out his keys and clicked. A BMW flashed its lights. He opened the passenger door for Louie and then folded himself into the front seat. Flooring it out of the parking garage, he merged into the noon traffic, reached into a console compartment, and grabbed a CD. He popped the disc from its casing and inserted it into the player. All of this one-handed as he tailgated a city cab. When the expressway signs appeared, Bradshaw pulled into the passing lane, cutting off a pickup.

"Idiot," shouted the driver.

"I should jam the brakes and teach that heathen a lesson, Louie," he sighed. "But ... we are all God's children. Better to turn the other cheek."

They headed south on the expressway. Louie gripped the armrest as Bradshaw accelerated. "I'm going to open this Beamer up, Louie. Blow out the impurities from the city."

The CD played *Rough an' Ready* by Whitesnake. "That's *Saints & Sinners* — one kick-ass album." He gunned the accelerator. "Best enjoyed at ninety miles an hour."

Louie blanched.

"Don't worry. I know each trooper patrolling this highway. Most of them are proud Latter-Day Saints ... or friends." He pushed the speedometer toward 100 mph. "Hold on to your hat, Louie."

• • • • •

"The Nevada desert," Bradshaw said as they passed a sign indicating Las Vegas 50 miles off. "Serpents, rocks, desolation. Yet, Sin City beckons on the horizon." He made a sharp right onto a dirt road, driving parallel to the state highway. "Just a few more miles, and ... Testimony Acres."

After minutes of lunar landscape, the Beamer screeched to a halt. "Here we are, Louie," Bradshaw said, leaving the car. He lifted his arm in a slow circular fashion, not unlike Vanna White unveiling a letter on Wheel of Fortune. "The heavy equipment arrives later this week."

"How come there's no tumbleweed or other vegetation, Leader Bradshaw?"

Bradshaw laughed. "This used to be an A-Bomb testing site. They say the folks in Vegas could see the mushroom cloud from the Strip. Imagine that." He bent over, scooped a pile of dirt, and held it in front of Louie, who took a slight step back. "Don't worry, Louie. We test it every few months. Hardly moves the Geiger counter."

He dropped the dirt, brushed his hands together, and patted Louie on the shoulder, leaving a light brown stain. "We break ground next week. You'll be staying at a local hotel and working out of a construction trailer." He laughed. "Don't worry, it will be air-conditioned."

Leaning into the passenger side on the BMW, he popped the glove compartment and withdrew a pack of cigarettes. He shook out a menthol, struck a match, and sucked it to life. He pointed the pack at Louie. "Want one?"

Louie shook his head.

"Good, Louie. These things will kill you." He laughed. "Plus, they're verboten for the brotherhood." He took a strong drag. "One of my peccadillos. I only smoke far away from headquarters."

He dropped the cigarette and crushed it with his shoe. Then, he dug a small hole with the toe of the same loafer and kicked the butt into it, covering it over with dirt. "Like it never happened, Louie."

He leaned against the door frame. "So, what do you think? Are you interested? This is a ground-level opportunity. Lots of money to be made all around. Our partners have deep pockets and are itching to convert their cash to real estate. If we do this right, it's a win-win. Our investors come out ahead, the LDS expands their Nevada holdings, and Leader Bradshaw, Bishop Warren, and Elder Kimball end up all the richer."

Louie thought this over. "Anything to help, Leader Bradshaw."

"Good, Louie. You'll be driving a Beamer before you know it."

CHAPTER 3

Louie stood on the wooden ramp outside the rusting trailer. *A hundred degrees, and it's only 9 a.m. Shit.* He surveyed Testimony Acres, its outline taking shape out of radioactive dirt, cheap labor, and the financial support of mysterious strangers.

Three men stood 100 yards away beside a Lincoln Town Car, waving their arms in animated conversation.

Marty Bradshaw's BMW pulled up. He hurried from the driver's side and shook each man's hand like he was pumping water from the parched ground. He motioned Louie over.

"Elder Louie Kimball. I don't believe you've met our key associates. Three gentlemen from the Community of Christ, the Reorganized LDS, if you will. We are all brothers in arms, though, hoping to spread the word, and, frankly, make money for our enterprises. They're here to see the progress you're making."

Bradshaw turned to the men. "With your financing, Testimony Acres will be ready for discriminating buyers in just a year or two. Louie here is cracking the whip, making sure labor and supplies stream into this yellow wasteland to be converted into luxury estates."

One man removed his sunglasses and squinted at Louie. "I'm Jared. I hope you understand our need for privacy, Elder Kimball. Our money comes from sources equally interested in anonymity."

He turned toward a heavyset man seeming to suffer from the heat. "This is Isaiah, our bookkeeper. He will be helping with the accounting for this project. You'll be working closely with him. He can train you in our techniques."

The third visitor pulled a handkerchief from his pocket and patted his brow. "And this is Carlos, our head of security," Jared said. "He'll make sure you're not distracted from your work by any outside influences."

Louie glanced around. "We're in the middle of nowhere, Jared. Not sure there will be many outside influences."

Bradshaw cleared his throat. "Louie, these men are well versed in business. Trust them. They've done this before." He opened the passenger side of his BMW and pulled out a red and white cooler. He struggled with the weight as he dropped it to the ground. Pulling the lid, he uttered a theatric "Ta da. Blue Moon, gentlemen. Chilled and ready for a desert thirst."

He leaned into the car again and removed a long leather bag, pointing it at the men. They flinched, each reaching inside his coat pocket. "Oh, no, gentlemen. Nothing dangerous here."

Bradshaw unzipped the case. Steam came out. "Ahhh. A four-foot-long Philly mushroom cheesesteak. With fried onions. There's a shop in Salt Lake City. Philly transplants." The men relaxed.

"Now let's go inside the trailer, destroy this bad boy, and pop a few of these brews before we get down to business."

CHAPTER 4

Isaiah saved the accounting spreadsheet on his laptop, stood in the modular trailer that served as their office, stretched, and reached for his Testimony Acres hat. "Another week in the books, Louie." He looked around at their cramped surroundings. "I'm glad the weekend is here. I'm getting cabin fever in this confined space."

Louie leaned over Isaiah's laptop. "Maybe I should double-check your numbers. Two sets of eyes are better than one."

Isaiah pushed up his sleeve and wrenched his head, squinting at his Rolex. "Four-fifteen, Louie. I can still make it to Vegas, hit the blackjack tables for a few hours, find an enormous steak, and head back to the hotel." He glared at Louie, who sat back and checked his watch to break the tension.

"A cheap timepiece there, Louie. You need more pizzazz in your life."

He took out a handkerchief and polished the face of his watch. "Funny story about this beauty. A business associate couldn't pay his bill. Seems he was running short on his luck." Isaiah removed it and placed it on the desk in front of Louie. "I said, 'Gimme your Rolex and we're square.' He suggested a payment plan, but I liked his watch." He snorted. "I guess he had sentimental reasons to keep it. His friggin' mistake. I was fond of it myself."

Isaiah pulled out a small switchblade. "A Buck 110, Louie. I call it my *negotiator*." He picked up the watch. "So, I say to him, 'You can give me the Rolex, or I can take it from your wrist as you bleed to death." Isaiah checked the wall clock to make sure both were in sync and slipped the timepiece over his wrist. "The guy decides that his health outweighs any sentimental value and graciously hands it over."

He reached for his car keys. "I don't enjoy being so direct in my interactions, but sometimes you gotta do what you gotta do."

He closed the lid of his laptop. "Now take my spreadsheets. They account for every transaction, some you're familiar with, others a bit more obscure. But it all balances out. No need for oversight from a kid who's still wet behind the ears. Trust me, Louie. It's better for the health of all involved if I keep the books and use my trusted accounting techniques."

Isaiah removed his tie, jammed it into his pocket, thought a second, and then placed the laptop into his satchel. "Capisce?"

Louie capisced.

●   ●   ●   ●   ●

Isaiah placed his suit coat and satchel in the back of his SUV, popped the sunroof, started the engine, and set the A/C to full blast. He glanced into his rearview. Louie was watching from the window.

He reached for his favorite CD: Tosca. "Take me out of this hellhole, Giacomo."

●   ●   ●   ●   ●

Louie picked up his cell, thought a few moments, then called Leader Bradshaw. "Marty, how's it going? Listen, Isaiah makes me nervous. He seems to have his own accounting rules. Are you sure our partners are on the up and up?"

Silence, then a sigh. "Louie, we don't normally associate with the Community of Christ, but this project is too big, and they have inroads to Nevada interests that we don't have." Marty cleared his throat loud enough to make Louie hold the phone away from his ear. "Just keep working and leave these guys to me."

CHAPTER 5

The printer chugged away as Isaiah whistled an unfamiliar tune. He returned from the back room and presented Louie with a quarterly expense summary.

He leafed through it as the accountant stood over him. "No need to go over it line by line, Louie. I vouch for the figures myself."

Louie sat back and drummed his fingers.

"Listen. It's simple. Just sign and date the last page."

I'll sign it. Just let me make a copy for my records."

The man turned red, then took a deep breath. "C'mon, Louie. Tell you what. How about if I keep a copy for both of us. It's easier that way."

Louie saw entries that seemed out of line with his understanding of construction costs. He moved his finger down the page and stopped at a line item. "I don't remember some of these expenses. Plus, there's a $500 consulting fee here. I don't recognize the name."

Isaiah frowned and said nothing. Louie worked his way further through the spreadsheet while hearing Isaiah's breathing rise in intensity. He looked up. Isaiah was polishing his Buck 110. Louie decided to sign on the dotted line.

"Don't forget to date it. Otherwise, it isn't considered kosher."

He added the date. "Will Leader Bradshaw get a chance to see these figures?" he asked. "I want to make sure he's OK with these numbers."

"Jared will present this report personally to Leader Bradshaw," Isaiah said. "After all, this is an LDS enterprise. We're just reorganizing things to see after our interests, and the overall success of Testimony Acres."

Isaiah picked up the signed report. "Tell you what, Louie. Let's call it a day and head out to Vegas. Gotta see my girlfriend again. I'm so horny, I could hump a cactus." He laughed. "If any could grow around here in this nuclear wasteland."

He put the knife into his pocket and report into his satchel. "She has a friend who, I'm sure, would take a shine to a young professional such as yourself." He swung Louie around and leaned in, grabbing each arm of the metal office chair.

"Ever see the movie *Scarecrow,* Louie? Gene Hackman and Al Pacino, prisoners in a dangerous correctional institute. The Hackman character takes the young Pacino under his wing. 'A man's gotta be regular,' he tells his protégé. Meaning, it's better to get some relief, rather than let things simmer up inside."

Isaiah stood and put on his suit coat. "Let's blow off some steam before you let all that tension cause you to make bad decisions."

Louie sighed, stood, and put on his jacket. "Lead the way."

Isaiah tossed the Explorer keys to Louie. "I'll let you drive. I need to fill Jared in on our plans. I'm sure he'll approve our little diversion."

CHAPTER 6

The next morning, Louie awoke in the work trailer, thirsty, hungry, and disheveled. *I don't remember getting to my hotel room last night. And how did I get into the office? Shit, what happened?*

He stood, stretched, and threw up in his mouth. He hurried to his small, barely ventilated bathroom, pushed open the window, and spit the foul liquid into the toilet. Rinsing his mouth, he flushed, put the lid down, and sat, holding his head.

A loud rap on the door. "Hey, Louie, are you gonna sleep all morning?" shouted Isaiah. "C'mon, we have a full day of work ahead of us. These houses aren't going to build themselves."

Crap, now I remember. Vegas. He turned to the mirror and saw himself, ragged, one day older, in serious need of a shave, and maybe, he thought, forgiveness. The same clothes he wore yesterday. A bit more wrinkled, and lipstick on his front shirttail?

Another knock.

"Give me a few minutes, Isaiah."

A laugh loud enough to frighten Louie. "So, my friend, sounds like you had as good a time as me. I gotta tell you, you made quite an impression on Brenda's friend, Candy, last night." He snorted. "Last I remember before Brenda and I went off for some private time, Candy was pulling on your shirt, and trying to unzip your pants with her teeth."

Louie winced as the "meep-meep" of an earthmover backing up shot through his brain. "I'll be ready in a few minutes. I just need to wash up, and ..." He scanned the floor. "Find my boots."

"I'll make you a pick-me-up, Louie. A little hair of the dog." Laughter. "And a nice breakfast sandwich. You like pork roll with a sharp mustard?"

Louie hurried back to the toilet, barfing on the closed lid until he could raise it.

"You'll get used to the Vegas experience. Before you know it, it'll be second nature."

Heavy footsteps descended the rickety wooden stairs. "I'll see you in a few minutes. Carpe diem, young soldier."

●   ●   ●   ●   ●

Months passed. Testimony Acres was taking shape, while Louie continued to lose his way.

He and Isaiah drove to Vegas every Tuesday and Friday night. They set up Brenda and Candy in a two bedroom apartment off the strip, and furnished the love nest with cheap Vegas art, flat screen TVs, and enough liquor to chase away any memory of desert grime. Louie lost track of how many commandments he had violated, hoping he had time and opportunity later to make amends.

One night, while Isaiah and Brenda were at a Barry Manilow concert, Louie and Candy opted for Penn and Teller. They arrived early at the Rio and found a table at a small lounge near the theater. Louie ordered a Heineken; Candy opted for white wine.

"So, Louie, this is nice. I could get used to this. Entertainment, drinks, the easy life."

"You know, Candy, we've never talked about your roots. You know I'm from Salt Lake City and an LDS elder. Who is Candy Hastings?"

She sighed. "Just a small town girl from Cedar Rapids, Iowa," she said. "I came to Vegas to be a showgirl, maybe meet a Hollywood agent. Me and hundreds of others getting off buses from the Midwest." She took a long sip of her Chardonnay. "Did the senior bus tours, Rotary dinners, and anything I could book through my agency." She laughed.

"I was one of the lucky ones. Some girls jump back on the next bus to home, dreams crushed, knowing that their shot at the big time came and went."

She ran her finger around the edge of her glass, and smiled at the faint hum of vibration. "Maybe they're the lucky ones. They had the sense to go back where their real life was, probably married some knight in shining armor, joined 'new mom' groups, and thanked God they found someone who sees them as a person, not just a good time."

Louie shuddered. "And I'm guessing that's not me. The knight part, anyway. Look, Candy, what we have is great, though it must seem superficial. I'm just a guy from Salt Lake, hoping to pursue my calling."

He laughed. "I guess that doesn't seem to make sense, seeing how these last few months have gone. Maybe I'm sowing my wild oats, maybe I'm looking for something more immediate. Who knows? Just be sure that you're more than a quick visit to bed. I *do* think of you as a friend, someone I care about."

"Don't make me cry, Louie. My mascara will run." She noticed the doors to the theater open. "Let's have a few laughs tonight, and sort things out some other time. Neither of us is going to start wearing sackcloth and ashes any time soon. Let's enjoy what we have and hope for something better later on down the road."

•　　•　　•　　•　　•

Isaiah didn't waste time examining his life. "Carpe diem," he would shout whenever Louie questioned their lifestyle. "In a few months, Louie, we'll hand over the keys to Testimony Acres, collect a large bonus, and go on to further exploits. In the meantime, Carpe diem."

Louie kept quiet while Isaiah manipulated the spreadsheets and spent long periods on his cell phone with Jared, licenses and inspections officials, various levels of law enforcement, and even Marty Bradshaw.

As executive officer of Testimony Acres, Marty was decidedly hands-off. He and Jared would visit the site on occasion, but spend most of their time with Isaiah and Carlos. Attempts by Louie to insert himself into their whispered conversations were not welcomed.

Louie pulled Marty aside one day, during one of his rare visits, while Jared, Isaiah, and Carlos toured the grounds. "Marty, I'm losing control of the project, if I ever *had* control. Isaiah and Carlos go over the books and send me off to deal with construction issues. All I do is sign the quarterly reports, and even those are pushed under my nose for a quick signature." He lowered his voice. "I'm not sure these guys are on the up and up. I've seen line items that don't make any sense. For all I know, they may be skimming money."

Marty frowned and pushed Louie into the shadows. "Elder Kimball, are you questioning my management approach?"

"Not at all, Leader Bradshaw. I just wanted you to be aware of my concerns?"

"You're not too concerned to stop humping your Vegas whore and focus on The Lord's business, are you, Louie?" He straightened his tie. "Physician, heal thyself."

Louie leaned against the trailer. "You're right, Leader Bradshaw. I guess I've sinned before God and man."

"Now, now, you're a young man with lots of responsibilities, and an easy path to temptation. Don't take your failings too hard. Just buck up and finish this project off."

He put his hand on Louie's shoulder. "You have a bright future, Louie," he said. "And you'll receive a nice bonus after the project completes." He laughed. "Maybe you'll do well enough to make your girlfriend an honest woman."

CHAPTER 7

Louie drove into town on a hot, dusty Saturday afternoon, parked and walked into a Starbucks. *I can't believe this one horse town has a coffee house and a McDonald's. There can't be more than a couple hundred people living here.*

He read the menu on the busy overhead board: *Demi, Venti, Grande. Crap. Can't drink this stuff, anyway.* He laughed as other customers stared at him. "Why can't they just say small or large, folks? Really," he said, hoping to save the moment. *Fornication, gambling, drinking ... but no coffee for Elder Kimball.*

He ordered an Orange Mango Smoothie, then succumbed to a seductive piece of cake just waiting to be microwaved and ravished. He saw a discarded Las Vegas Sun scattered on a nearby table and opened to the Sports section. UNLV had landed a five-star recruit. *Good. Maybe he'll end up with the Jazz in a few years.*

The smoothie and cake arrived. Louie held the treat near his nose and inhaled. *Hah, cinnamon, yellow cake, and streusel, steaming and ready for its fate.* He removed the lid from the drink and sniffed again. *Mango, orange, vanilla. Heaven on earth.*

He stabbed the cake and, closing his eyes, took a long sensuous bite. When he reopened them, other patrons raised their drinks in salute. Louie sipped his smoothie and laughed with his fellow gastronomes. "Makes a Saturday afternoon worthwhile, don't you think?" he said to nods of agreement.

A man in a T-shirt displaying the Bellagio water fountains, balanced a ham and swiss panini, a bottle of water and a KIND bar as he searched for a table in the crowded shop. He stood by Louie. "Mind if I join you, young man? No other open tables."

Louie gestured to the empty chair across from him. The man dumped his items on the table, returned to the counter, and pulled a dozen napkins, one at a time, from the dispenser. He returned and sat. "I'm a messy eater. I'll probably use each of these guys before I'm done."

"Do you mind if I continue reading my paper?" Louie asked.

"Be my guest. I'll just quietly eat my meal."

The panini suffered indignity not normally doled out to a heated sandwich. The man finished it in four loud bites. When Louie looked up, the man was wiping tomato sauce and cheese from the Bellagio landmark.

"Gotta wash this guy, soon," he laughed. He guzzled the water and laid waste to the fruit and nut snack bar. He sat in silence as Louie finished his cake and smoothie. Louie carried his trash, and the man's, to the receptacle, sat again and opened his paper to the local news.

The man reached into his pocket and exposed a badge. "So, Elder Kimball," he said.

Louie sat back.

"Agent Nelson. FBI, Salt Lake City. We need to talk about your little desert project." He sat forward, returning his badge to his pocket. "Specifically, the books and your business partners."

The hipsters at the next table stared and whispered to each other.

"Let's do this downtown. More privacy there." He held out his hand. "Give me your keys. An associate will move your car to a safe place. Can't leave it outside a Starbucks for hours on end. Attracts too much attention." He looked out at Louie's pickup. "Tell you what. We'll get it washed for you, too."

CHAPTER 8

Louie hunched down in his seat as they passed the Church Office Building on the way to the FBI field office. Nelson laughed. "Don't worry, Kimball. We can work out a way to keep this quiet. No one has to know this happened. Not yet, anyway."

In a few minutes, he pulled into the parking garage, and showed his badge to the security guard. They drove into a nearby reserved spot. "The perks of seniority. For years, I was so far away I was puffing by the time I got to my office. Us desk jockeys aren't in the same shape as the young pups."

They entered the building and walked the hallway, passing through several sets of double doors. Nelson swiped his badge and put it back into his coat pocket. He laughed as Louie sighed and wiped sweat from his forehead. "Hey, why don't I just call you *Louie*? Don't worry, we won't be squeezing into a phone booth like Maxwell Smart." He turned into a small office and motioned to him. "Here we are. Want some coffee?"

Louie shook his head and sat. No whoopee cushion like Bishop Warren's office. Good. That would have been hard to take. "Agent Nelson, exactly why am I here?"

Nelson sat and turned on his laptop. "We've had an eye on Testimony Acres for a while, Louie. Creating a Xanadu out of literally thin air." He typed, then grunted. "Gotta change my password. They require a new one every 30 days." He sat back, studied the ceiling, lunged forward and typed. "Ok, this is one I'll remember."

He smiled. "It's funny, people hate passwords. They use whatever first comes to mind. Like no one will ever try to figure it out."

He squinted as his screen came back to life. "Now, where was I? Oh, yeah. Where's the LDS getting the front money? Are they passing the collection basket? I doubt it." He shifted in his seat and pulled down his Bellagio shirt to cover his ample belly. "It's cold in here, Louie. Normally, I'm better dressed."

He turned his laptop. "Then one day, Jared Benson arrives with his cohort." Jared's picture covers Nelson's screen. He pages down. "And his bookkeeper, Isaiah Young. Tall, sweaty guy. I believe an actual descendent of Brigham Young. Go figure."

He moved the screen to face away from Louie. "The third guy we had trouble identifying. Turns out he's Carlos Garcia. A Hispanic in the brotherhood." He started to show Louie the screen, then stopped. "You know what he looks like."

Reaching into a drawer, he removed a Payday bar, ripped it open, and took a few seconds to admire the masterpiece. "You want part of this, Louie? Those KIND bars can't match up."

"Can we move on, agent?"

Nelson took a healthy bite, and exposed a peanut crumb wedged between his front teeth. "OK. So, we have money from the Community of Christ, headed by Jared Benson and his group. Isaiah Young is doing the books, and Carlos Garcia is running security. Poor Kimball is the squeaky-clean site foreman, probably too dumb to know he's being set up in case the whole venture falls through."

He took another bite, sensed the wayward peanut and dislodged it with a paperclip. "Sound about right?"

•　　•　　•　　•　　•

The agent sat back as a technician removed the lie detector. "I'm glad you did this voluntarily. The detector isn't admissible in court, but it gives me a baseline for trusting you."

Louie pulled down his shirt cuffs. "What next?"

"As we suspected, you're the dupe in this whole gambit." Nelson opened another screen on his laptop. "Let me lay it out. We're looking at money laundering, bribery of public officials, and fraud. The Community of Christ, and your bosses Warren and Bradshaw, have been making a small fortune on Testimony Acres."

He closed the screen. "You became a person of interest once you started your twice weekly trips to Sin City. We know about the apartment, your girlfriend, and hedonism." He laughed. "Not exactly your missionary lifestyle."

Louie squirmed.

"Don't worry, Louie. If we arrested everyone who transgressed in Vegas, we'd need a prison as large as ..." He laughed, "Testimony Acres."

He stood, pulled up the blinds, and leaned on the window frame. He waved Louie over. "We can see them. They can't see us. On a Saturday afternoon, the usual bus tours, guided visits to the religious infrastructure, even folks doing ancestry searches in the Family History Library. No one suspecting that the church hierarchy is embezzling funds in the Church Office Building right down the street."

He closed the shades. "Boy, it's a hot one today. Must be a hundred." He motioned Louie to the guest chair, returned to his own, sat, and swiveled. "Louie, we're building a strong case against Warren, Bradshaw, and the Community. But we need the computer files that Isaiah Young is maintaining. This is where you come in."

He opened a drawer. "We'll give you a thumb drive and a burner phone. We need you to copy his files and hand the drive over to us. No need for a search warrant, since an officer of Testimony Acres, that's you, Louie, gave them to us voluntarily. Your contact number is on the burner. It's low on battery. Remember to keep it charged. Call that number when you've got the files."

He pulled out a squeeze ball and worked his left hand, then tossed it to his right and repeated. "Then, of course, you have to testify at trial. Lay out the whole history of Testimony Acres, and how Isaiah Young's questionable accounting techniques helped to fuel the criminal enterprise."

"Then I go to prison, anyway?"

"Normally you'd get 20 years, but don't worry. We'll drop any charges against you ... once you testify and your associates are convicted."

He put the ball down, sat back, and held up his hands together, framing Louie in a makeshift camera lens. "This is a big case. We'll put you in witness protection and send you far away. We'll also tweak your appearance, smooth out those rough edges."

The agent picked up the squeeze ball and tossed it to Louie. "So. Ready to play ball?"

CHAPTER 9

When he was dropped off at his hotel, Louie found his car, all shiny, and even detailed. He entered his room, opened a club soda, flopped into the worn sofa chair, and considered his options. Bishop Warren, Leader Bradshaw, Jared, Isaiah, and Carlos all stealing from the church, and worse, setting him up to take the fall. His faith was shaken, he was angry, but also realized he was in danger no matter what decision he made.

And here's Louie, prepped to take the fall. Louie the fine young man according to Bishop Warren. Louie the sinner according to Leader Bradshaw. More like Louie the schmuck.

I can't take the rap for this, yet can I turn against my upbringing? He prayed for guidance. No easy answers. Cooperating with the FBI would mean his current life would be over. He'd never see Candy again, and probably have to start over, somewhere far away.

Bastards. You can't trust anyone. He decided to work with Nelson, the lesser of many evils. He studied himself in the mirror. *Crap. And I do look like a ferret: angular face, bushy eyebrows, close-set eyes. What else can go wrong with my life?*

How would he get the files for the FBI? Not an easy task since Isaiah was never far from his laptop. *I just need 15 minutes where he's distracted and I can dump the files on to this thumb drive. Then resume my day with him none the wiser.*

He picked up his Starbucks personalized cup, 'Louie' inscribed below the mermaid symbol. *The mermaid resembles Donna, the barista. Flowing hair, teasing smile. Built like a brick shithouse.*

Always flirting for tips. She even passed me her number. In case I got <u>lonely and needed comfort</u>, she said. Well, I'm more lonely than ever, now. His eyes widened at a new thought. *Maybe she can help me with Isaiah.* He dialed, hoping for an answer before he lost his nerve.

"Hello."

"Donna. It's me, Louie Kimball. Remember me from the store?"

Silence. "Oh, the young guy who looks like a f..., I mean, yes, Louie. How are you?"

"It's a lonely Saturday night. I'm lonely. Can we meet up?"

"Sure. Stop by my place. Desert Apartments, Number 57C. I'll see you soon.. Oh, yeah. I prefer cash. Credit cards are so icky."

"I'll be there in an hour, Donna. I'll bring plenty of money." He paused and thought over his plan. "In fact, I have a business proposition for you if you're free Monday morning. Easy money. I'll fill you in later."

•   •   •   •   •

Donna knew things. Very efficient. Within 10 minutes of knocking on her door, Louie was no longer lonely and in need of comfort. He watched Donna dress, and explained his proposal. "At 11 a.m. Monday, fake a breakdown on the highway just outside the construction entrance to Testimony Acres. Wear something that will make you get noticed. Think the car washing scene in *Cool Hand Luke*.

In a few minutes, a tall, sweaty man will come out of the trailer and offer his assistance. You're so overcome by his offer to help and his animal magnetism that soon you're inside your van with him, getting to know each other better. Take your time with him. Just make sure you're the only thing on his mind."

She stopped dressing. "So, I get to act in addition to comforting him? You know, I'm really a dramatic actress waiting for my big break." She smiled. "This might be fun."

"There's five hundred in it for you. I believe that's way beyond scale given to young actresses."

"You got a deal, director. Monday at eleven."

CHAPTER 10

Monday morning. Isaiah entered the trailer around a quarter of eleven, unpacked his laptop and loosened his tie. "How was your weekend, Louie? I finally got some sleep. Can't burn the candle at both ends all the time."

"It was low key, Isaiah. A trip into town, lunch, some personal business."

Isaiah powered on his laptop. "Password, password. Oh, yeah. How could I forget?" He typed the code, stood, and walked over to the stove. "Another week in the salt mine, eh, Louie? Now, where's my mug?"

He found his Tasmanian Devil cup, the brown whirlwind showing an evil, toothy grin. Isaiah emptied four sugar packets and a waterfall of artificial creamer into the cup, followed by the molten, two-hour-old pot of Pero. He took a sip and winced. "Man, this is terrible. We believers need to lighten up on coffee."

Louie shrugged. "A sign of self-control, Isaiah. We need to prove our mettle."

The big man laughed. "I guess so. We at least need to keep up appearances."

He lifted his cup. "Carpe diem."

A knock on the door. Carlos. "Hey, Isaiah and Louie. There's a broken down van along the roadway. Catch a sight of the driver. A real looker. And she's hardly wearing anything."

The men opened the door and the three stared at the disabled motorist. "Wow, look at that," Isaiah said. "She's gonna get one hell of a sunburn."

He nudged his enforcer. "She needs a knight in shining armor, Carlos." He turned to Louie and laughed. "I need to show her my mettle."

Carlos left to continue his rounds. Isaiah straightened his tie, smoothed his shirt, and put on his Testimony Acres cap. He started to walk down the construction entrance over to the highway. "Be back in a few, Louie."

Louie watched as Isaiah walked across the dirt road and on to the shoulder of the two-lane highway. He waited for traffic to pass, waved to Donna, and hurried to the van. He tipped his cap. *Very gallant.* Louie closed the door, parted the curtains, and viewed out the grimy window. Isaiah peeked under the hood, reached inside and fiddled with something. He motioned Donna to start the van. It came to life.

She jumped out and thanked her rescuer, pecking him on the cheek. He doffed his cap again, and pointed to the engine, no doubt explaining his adjustment. Donna leaned in closer to see for herself, her hair brushing against Isaiah's stubble. She turned, grabbed his face with both hands and kissed him so hard, Isaiah had to hold on to the grill for balance.

Taking his hand, she led him into the back of the van. After a few moments, the van started rocking. Louie walked over to the desk, slightly hunched from his unexpected erection. He reached for the memory stick.

He found a USB port and plugged in. "Crap, it's password protected. What now?" he mumbled. He sat back and stared out at the van. Still rocking.

Louie sat silent. *What's an easy password for Isaiah to remember.* After a minute, he smiled and typed "carpediem." The screen came to life.

•   •   •   •   •

Louie finished the file dump in 15 minutes. He removed the thumb drive, put it in his pocket, and returned to his desk. He checked the window. Still rocking. *Atta boy, Isaiah. Keep it going until the system prompts again for the password.*

A knock on the door. "Hey, it's Carlos. You guys getting lunch?"

"How about in a half hour or so, Carlos? I have a few things to finish up. Besides, I think Isaiah is still helping the damsel in distress."

Silence, then a laugh. "Look at that van rock. Our friend must have an unlimited supply of testosterone." Carlos lumbered down the stairs. "I'll check with you again in a half hour. He can't last forever."

"If he does, he'll have to give us pointers," Louie replied.

Twenty minutes later, slow steps on the stairs. Louie opened the door. Isaiah, one hand on the railing, catching his breath. "You OK, Isaiah?"

The man limped into the trailer. "Couldn't be better. What's in that Pero, anyway?"

He flopped into his chair. "That … was great." He glanced out the window. Donna, wearing the Testimony Acres cap, was driving off. "See, Louie. You do a good deed and you get paid back tenfold." He laughed. "Actually, it was twice, but it felt like ten times."

He opened the lid to his laptop. "Carpeeeeee friggin' diem," he said as he typed. "Seize the day."

Carlos knocked on the door. "Who's ready for lunch?"

CHAPTER 11

Louie, Isaiah, and Carlos sat in Wendy's. Louie could feel the memory stick in his pocket, like the knife just used to stab Caesar. The men watched ESPN on a large flat screen as they devoured burgers, fries, and chicken nuggets. The Jazz had pummeled the Nets last night, and the highlights were on.

"Man, those Nets never have a good team," said Isaiah. "I thought they'd improve after all this time. Maybe it's the Jersey air."

Carlos put down his double bacon cheeseburger. "Guys, let's not disparage Jersey. I have relatives there. It's not a bad place once you get south enough and away from the congestion."

"Name one good team they have, Carlos," Isaiah said. "The Jets, The Giants, also-rans. The Devils were good for a while, but now they're just so-so. At least the Vegas Knights are the class of hockey."

Louie played with his chili. "What's up with you, Louie?" Isaiah said. "You look like you have the weight of the world on your shoulders."

He forced a smile. "Just having a hard time sleeping lately." He gestured to the window. "Maybe if it wasn't a hundred degrees all day long."

"Jersey," Carlos said, waving a fry. "You get the ocean breezes, the salt air, and the boardwalk. Nothing like this solar surface. You gotta go there someday, Louie."

"Someday, I guess," Louie said. He examined his watch. "I have to get back and check on the Salvation section. The plumbers are behind."

Isaiah and Carlos crammed their remaining lunch into their mouths, sipped their drinks and stood. "Good idea," Isaiah said. "Besides, I need a little siesta after my morning interaction with the young lady." He laughed. "There's only so much gas in the tank."

They returned in Carlos' Humvee. Louie and Isaiah stretched as they emerged. "Must be a hundred ten," said Carlos. He put on his Testimony Acres cap. "Hopefully, we can finish up this project soon, and head for a better climate."

He left, heading toward the security stations. Isaiah went into the trailer, then into the back bedroom, judging from the sound of squeaky springs reacting to an unexpected weight. Louie opened his pickup, gasped as the heat from the steering wheel almost blistered his skin, and drove toward the Salvation section. Checking that he wasn't followed. He turned off and left the site, driving toward town.

He found a Chevron station, filled the tank, bought a Hershey bar, and paid the clerk, Linda. He parked in a spot away from the store and opened the burner phone. Battery at zero percent and starting to shut down. *Crap, I forgot to charge it.* He scribbled the contact number on a napkin and considered his next move.

He saw a pay phone by the highway. *Gotta do it.* He returned to the store, asked for change of a dollar, and walked to the booth. He checked for anyone passing nearby, wiped off the greasy mouthpiece, and dialed a number provided by the FBI. "I have the information Agent Nelson requested," he said to his contact. "When can I hand it over to you? Six, at McDonald's? OK."

•   •   •   •   •

Louie returned to the trailer, still feeling his pocket for the drive. *Tonight, I give this thing to my contact and it's out of my hands. Why do I feel so dirty? These guys are ripping off the LDS and the general public. Still, it feels like a betrayal.*

Isaiah emerged from the back room and stretched his arms. "I feel like a new man, Louie. Ready to tackle anything. Carpe diem!"

CHAPTER 12

Louie stood and stretched. "I'm done for the day, Isaiah. I'm going to get some dinner, and call it an early night."

"OK. I have a few things I need to take care of before I leave. See you tomorrow."

He patted his right pocket as he descended the wooden steps,. The stick was still there, ready for handing over. He slid into the pickup and started the engine. Carlos walked in front of the truck and held up a hand. "I need to talk to you, Louie," he shouted above the noise from the engine.

He walked to the driver's side door and had Louie roll down the window. "I saw you leave by the side entrance after lunch. Caught you on the monitor."

Louie drummed the steering wheel, took a breath, and started to respond. "Remember what I told you, Isaiah, and the crew?" Carlos continued. "I prefer that you leave by the front entrance. It's easier to account for the comings and goings."

"Sorry, Carlos. When I noticed I was short on gas, I took the first exit and headed into town. I'll be more careful in the future."

"Make sure you are, Louie. We need to run a tight ship here. Can't have people run off without being noticed."

"OK, Carlos."

"Hey, where'd you get gas? I need to fill up myself."

"I went to the Chevron station down the road."

"Hey, was that knockout Linda behind the counter?" He laughed. "A pleasant diversion in this barren desert."

"Yeah, Carlos. A nice lady."

"OK, on your way, Louie. Have a good evening."

●　　●　　●　　●　　●

Carlos left an hour later. Driving to the Chevron station, he saw Linda getting into her car. He honked and parked beside her. "Hi, Linda. Done for the day?"

The woman leaned out. "Yeah, Carlos. Jenna is on duty now. Picking up a few things?"

He started his engine. "I was gonna gas up. Louie Kimball said he was here earlier and you were on duty."

"Yeah, nice guy," Linda said. "After he filled up, he got change for a buck and made a phone call from the booth by the road. Must have a hot date."

Carlos thought this over. "OK, Linda. Have a good evening." She drove off.

"I wonder why he called from a pay phone," Carlos mumbled. "He could have called from his cell."

●　　●　　●　　●　　●

Louie drove into town as dusk settled in. He parked in the McDonald's lot and hurried past motorists leaving the drive-thru. *Man, where are all these people from? And why can't they wait for a guy to actually go inside?*

He carried his tray, balancing a Big Mac, giant fries, and a large shake, to a table in the corner. He pulled out his phone, swiped to Candy Crush Saga, and sipped his drink. The thick fluid refused to pass through. Disposing of the lid and straw, he took a gulp.

On the large screen TV, a *Cops* episode played catchy music as officers in dark uniforms swarmed a house. Inside, a bald, disheveled guy sipped a beer and watched a sitcom, the canned laughter audible to those waiting to rush in.

Boom! The door splinters and the SWAT team attacks. The man takes another sip, like this happens every day.

They start to drag him away, two of them struggling to wrestle the Bud from his hand. His wife, from appearances, comes forward and shouts obscenities at her husband. The guy seems somehow relieved that he'll spend the night elsewhere.

"Hey, buddy. You got shake around your mouth," said a man standing next to Louie's table. He put a few napkins next to Louie's Big Mac. "Here, use these."

Louie studied him for a second, picked up a napkin, and wiped his lips as the new acquaintance sat at the next table. Reaching into his pocket, Louie looked around and, seeing no one watching, placed the thumb drive under the remaining napkins. "I got it, thanks. You can have the rest back." He placed the pile next to the man's McNuggets and Coke.

He finished his meal, dumped his trash, and walked out, not looking back. As he started to pull out, Carlos drove into the lot and honked. Louie peed himself, just a little.

"Hey, Louie. Imagine finding you here. What's the blue plate special today?" Carlos laughed as he walked over to Louie. "Hey, you got some ketchup on your chin."

Louie wiped the condiment with his hand.

"I gassed up at the Chevron, myself, Louie. I saw Linda just as she left for the day. She said you made a call from the pay phone there. Why didn't you use your cell?"

Louie peed himself some more. "Low battery. I guess I play too many games. Anyway, I was just checking the movie times."

"What's playing?"

Louie thought a second. "*Jurassic Park,* of all things. Running on four screens."

Carlos squinted at Louie as if expecting to read his mind. "That's an oldie, but I love that movie. Enjoy the show."

Louie, relieved that he had seen the marquis when driving in this morning, settled into his truck. *I guess I'm seeing Jurassic Park tonight.*

He adjusted his rearview mirror and watched Carlos walk into the McDonald's. He passed a man emptying his tray of his nuggets and coke. The men nodded to each other.

•　　•　　•　　•　　•

The next morning, Isaiah walked up the trailer stairs, and fiddled with the door as he held a bag of donuts, and a small coffee. The door opened seemingly on its own, Isaiah juggling his breakfast as the handle was wrested from his hand. Carlos stood inside, his hand clutching the knob.

Isaiah regained control of his breakfast, climbed over the last step, and laid his bags on his desk. "Well, you caught me, Carlos. I need caffeine once in a while or I get the heebie-jeebies." He laughed. "Don't tell Louie."

"That's OK, Isaiah. Spirit willing, flesh weak."

Carlos sat in the visitor chair as the man added sugar and creamer. He stirred until some of the hot liquid spilled over the side, onto his hand. "Damn, that's hot," he said as he sucked the liquid, making sure to not lose a drop. "So, what's up my friend?"

Carlos sighed and started to talk.

"Wanna donut, Carlos?" said his host, interrupting.

"That's OK, Isaiah," he responded. "Had some oatmeal earlier."

"Ouch. This must seem like I've lost my self-control. Don't worry, Carlos. I intend to lose a few pounds later on, after I finish the books on Testimony Acres."

Carlos shrugged. "You know, Isaiah, as head of security, I monitor the entrances and exits. Yesterday, Louie took a side exit, then drove to the Chevron to gas up. *Then*, he gets change for a buck and makes a phone call from that scuzzy phone booth off of the highway."

Isaiah took a bite of his Boston cream donut. He sat back and pondered this information as filling stuck to his cheek. "Did you have a chance to ask him about this?"

"He said he was checking movie times, though that sounded fishy to me."

Carlos pointed to his friend's cheek. Isaiah checked his reflection in his laptop screen, found the filling, swiped it with his pointer finger, and slurped the cream down.

"He identified *Jurassic Park* as the movie, which was right, so he may have been telling the truth. Still, I don't know. Seems suspicious."

Isaiah took a sip of his brew and spun back and forth in his chair. A pickup pulled up outside. "That's him," Isaiah said. "Get back to work, Carlos. I'll take it from here."

As Carlos opened the door, Louie stood holding a smoothie and a bear claw, fumbling with his keys. "Thanks, Carlos. I expected trouble." He brushed past the big man, feeling his hot breath. He put the pastry on his desk. "I know. Not good for me. I'll atone for this later."

Carlos frowned at Louie, then shrugged. "I guess we all need to atone once in a while." He slid past but then turned. "So, how was the movie?"

Louie lost color, then laughed. "Same old story. God creates dinosaurs ... God destroys dinosaurs ... Man creates dinosaurs."

Reaching for his keys, Carlos grunted. "The penalty for interfering with the natural order of things." He pressed the auto start, his Humvee roaring to life. "Best not to mess with powers beyond our control, Louie. Things could get out of hand."

•   •   •   •   •

Louie sat and mulled over Carlos's advice. *Am I over my head here, preparing to turn state's evidence?* He bit into the pastry and sipped his smoothie, sitting back to enjoy the rush, he bent forward. *Damn, brain freeze.* He rubbed his temple as he winced in pain.

Isaiah laughed. "You gotta be careful with that stuff, Louie. Makes you think your head is imploding."

He crab-walked in his rolling chair and stopped next to his associate. "So, you told me you were calling it an early day yesterday. What made you decide to see a movie instead? A sudden urge to see predator and prey go at it? The good guys don't always win, Louie. Best not to expect to tip the balance."

"I didn't want to stare at four walls in my motel room. It's not exactly the Ritz Carlton."

Isaiah broke off a piece of Louie's breakfast, took a bite, and grabbed his coffee, reaching across the common table. He took a long sip. "You're a fine young man, Louie. A good worker, and, I hope, a loyal follower. Just a few more months of this project, then we can hand it off to others."

He took another sip, making a slurping noise that unsettled Louie. "Best not to disturb the progress we're making."

He put his arm around Louie. "What I'm saying is, keep your nose to the ground and your mouth shut. It's healthier that way. And no more highway phone calls." He pointed to the smoothie. "You think a quick headache is bad, it's nothing compared to a knife in the ribs."

He wheeled back to his side of the desk. "Now, back to work."

CHAPTER 13

A month went by. No further word from the FBI, which was OK with Louie. Maybe there was nothing in the files to bring charges. Another month and he could go back to Salt Lake City while his replacement put the final touches on the construction. Bishop Warren said there were big things ahead for him.

He wouldn't mind if he just returned to ringing doorbells and spreading God's word. No more Vegas, drinking, and debauchery. He'd miss Candy. He wasn't in love, but they had this comfortable, no-strings relationship that had grown into friendship.

Isaiah stretched and yawned as he opened a map and moved his finger down the page. "Just one day 'til the weekend, Louie. Brenda wants to go see Red Rocks Canyon. Not sure why. You've seen one stretch of desert, you've seen it all."

No point in debating. Isaiah would be half wasted, anyway.

"So how about you, Louie? Brenda says Candy is out of town, visiting her folks." He laughed. "I guess it's too early to introduce her LDS boyfriend."

"We're taking it slow, Isaiah. Appreciating each other and having a good time."

"Wish I could say I'm jealous, Louie," Isaiah said. "But Brenda and I are still in the 'Slam, Bam, Thank You, Ma'am' part of our relationship, and it's fine with both of us."

Sirens and red lights interrupted their talk. "Get down, fella. FBI."

"What's going on here," yelled Carlos. "I'm head of security. You just can't barge in."

"Down on the ground and keep quiet. Agent, cuff him!"

Footsteps ascended the steps to the trailer, then "FBI. Stand back." The door opened with such force that it banged against a Ficus in the corner and toppled it. Nelson walked in followed by men with rifles. "Hands out and on the table, gentlemen. This is a raid. We have a warrant to search the premises."

"What are you looking for," Isaiah said as agents frisked him and Louie.

"You're under arrest for mail fraud, money laundering, and related charges." He turned to his agents. "Take them away and keep them separate."

Louie tried to make eye contact, but the agent ignored him as he reached for Isaiah's uneaten chocolate chip muffin. "These things will kill you, buddy," he said to Isaiah as they led him away. He sniffed. "Hmm, still warm. And greasy, I bet"

Agents drove off with Isaiah and Carlos, as others loaded Louie into a van. Nelson sat in front, wrote a note, and turned to him. "Had to make it look like a complete takedown. In fact, we need to keep you in custody while we see what we come up with here." He clicked the pen. "I have to say that your information was helpful. It connected a lot of dots and implicated members of the church leadership."

He turned to the front. "Let's go, Jim. Let's get this guy processed and away from the lawyers until we can get things tied up." He adjusted the rearview to see his informant. "You did a good thing, Kimball. These were bad men. They're going away for a long time."

Louie sighed and closed his eyes.

"We'll put you into protective custody during the trial and then witness protection." He laughed. "Once we correct that facial issue of yours. Must not have been easy going through life looking like that."

CHAPTER 14

The next six months dragged by for Louie: relentless questioning from the FBI, meeting with "fixers" who worked on a new life story for their prize witness, and even a surgeon who twisted his face, examining the landscape for every angle and flaw.

"Think of me as your personal portrait artist, Louie," the doctor said. "Someone who's going to take the rough edges, and sculpt a newer, unrecognizable Louie Kimball. Of course, you won't be *Kimball* anymore. Just an average Joe. Be assured, though, when I'm done, your own mother wouldn't recognize you."

"No need for that, doc. My mother and father are gone, on to their reward knowing that they raised a son who would do them proud and carry on the religious tradition." He laughed. "I guess I didn't turn out quite as they expected."

The doctor gestured around the small medical office in the basement of the FBI building. "Do any of us? This isn't exactly the Mayo Clinic."

"I guess we make our own destiny," Louie said.

"Exactly. Better to look forward to a new life than to beat yourself up about the past."

●　　　●　　　●　　　●　　　●

United States District Court. Salt Lake City, Utah. Louie fidgeted in the cold, small room. Bobby, the guard, smiled at him. "They keep it at 65 in the courthouse. A lot of people can heat up an old building like this."

Louie started to walk to the window. "I wouldn't do that, Mr. Kimball. We keep it secure, but you never know who will take a pot shot, especially one at a marked man such as yourself."

The guard closed the shades. "Now, don't worry about me, mind you. I'm a Catholic. We're rare as hen's teeth in Utah, but we comprise a decent portion of the federal civil service. Wouldn't reflect well on the church if you were to take a bullet, especially on my shift."

A loud knock. Louie shook and leaned on the table to get his balance.

The guard went to the reinforced metal door. "Yeah, Mike. What is it?"

A voice on the other side said, "Agent Nelson is here to talk to our guest."

He had Louie sit, then opened the door. Nelson walked in. "Hi, Bobby. How's our guest holding up?"

"A little anxious, Agent. I guess I would be too if I screwed over those people."

"Now, now. Mr. Kimball performed a real service to the people of Utah, and the citizens of the United States. Larceny, bribery of public officials, accounting fraud, you name it. Warren, Bradshaw, and their associates are going away for a long time."

He sat and studied Louie, who was pale, sweating slightly even in this cold room, and staring at the chipped Formica table. "Kimball, with your help, we got conviction on all the major counts. You performed well, even if it was in exchange for us dropping your charges and putting you into witness protection. We'll sneak you out the side door, and away to a safe house."

"What then?" asked Louie, finally making eye contact.

"We'll make your new identity official, and arrange for a new life, far away from here." He motioned Bobby to go outside and join his colleague. "Kimball, I doubt you have many friends left in Salt Lake City. In fact, our moles are saying that you're a marked man with a reward on his head. So, the transition to a new life far, far, away is really the only choice."

He winced, examining Louie's face like a geologist studying topology. "We scheduled the operation to change your appearance." Nelson sat back. "I spoke to the doctor. A nip here, a tuck there. All healed in a few weeks. We'll also work on your Utah dialect. Not too severe, fortunately, but they'll smooth it out. Believe me, Kimball, after we're done, no one will recognize you."

He pulled out a map and unfolded it on the table. "Now for your new home. How does southern New Jersey sound? Not too many Believers there."

PART 2
TOWN CENTRE

CHAPTER 15

Long Harbor, New Jersey. Three Years Later
Hank Malone opened the paper bag, placed his face over the top and inhaled so hard the paper collapsed inward. "Ah," he whispered as steam escaped. "Cranberry orange with nuts." He placed the muffin on a plastic plate and studied the masterpiece.

He pulled the lid from his large Columbian coffee, repeated the sniff test. *I can't believe I lived the first 29 years of my life without this stuff.*

Mixing the brew, he opened the Saturday edition of The Long Harbor Press to the Sports section. He read the headline: 'Predators Looking for a Winning Season.' Hank grunted. *They better. Those season tickets are expensive.*

The doorbell rang. Hank stopped stirring and waited a few seconds, maintaining a strict silence, hoping they would go away. It rang again. He dropped the paper and leaned forward to part the curtains enough to view his unwanted visitors: three men in white shirts, dark slacks, and thin tie. The taller one in the middle saw him and waved his hand. Hank sat back, the shade remaining open. *Crap.*

The doorbell again. "The Church of The Latter-Day Saints, sir," a voice called out. "Can we tell you about God's plan for your salvation?"

"No, thanks," Hank shouted. "I'm busy right now." He awaited a response. "Can you just leave something in my mail slot?"

A face appeared in the windowpane, the glass steaming up from the breath of the missionary. "Hello. I'm Elder Nick Olsen. We'll leave our pamphlets, sir," he shouted to be heard through the glass. "Very informative. They can show you the path to everlasting happiness."

Hank turned away. "OK. Gotta go now."

"Have a joy-filled day, sir."

The three men walked to the sidewalk as Hank watched from the window. Elder Olsen stopped and turned toward the rancher, scratched his head, then continued on.

•   •   •   •   •

Hank waited for the men to disappear from view. He pulled his phone, opened his contacts, broke off a piece of the muffin and chewed. "Shit," he mumbled. "I hate to just pack up and leave."

He sipped his coffee. *"I can't call Benner yet. He'll have me out of here in no time. No goodbye to Sue, no last beer with my buddies. Long Harbor will be in my rearview mirror before I realize it.*

He picked up his car keys, reached for his jacket, and walked to the garage. His pickup started after a few coughs and sputters and Hank eased out of the driveway, coasting down the street, seeking the three men. He spotted them and continued past as they walked toward a late model Ford. The tall one, Elder Olsen, slid his thin frame into the driver's side as his companions climbed in opposite.

Hank pulled over and watched the men as they drove off. Jotting down the license plate, he made a U-turn and returned home.

•   •   •   •   •

"I'm sorry, Hank. I just can't call in a license unless you give me a good reason. Do you have any concern that your cover is blown?"

Hank thought this over. "No, Charlie. The creep cut me off in traffic and I want to know who it is."

"Well you can call the local police if you want," Charlie Benner said. "But frankly, if I were you, I'd suck it up and let it go. The more invisible you are, the better."

"OK," Hank said, picking at his muffin. "I guess you're right. Sorry to bother you. Good bye."

He sipped his coffee and gagged on the cold and sugary liquid. He dumped his breakfast into the trash, and slumped in his chair, staring at the ceiling. *Maybe it's nothing. They must see dozens of people every day. I don't stand out.*

Remembering the pamphlets, he walked to his front door and saw the glossy brochures on the floor beneath his mail slot. He examined each, then saw a business card identifying a meeting house on Federal Street in Camden. He sat at his laptop and searched for 'Mormons in Camden.'

So, the LDS have formed a ward in South Jersey, Great. And they're proselytizing in Long Harbor of all places. Maybe I should call Charlie back.

His phone warbled and he checked the ID: Sue. He took a calming breath and answered. "Hi, Sue. I thought you were on your shift at the hospital." He checked his watch. "You want to meet for lunch, at Giorgio's? Sure. See you there at 1."

He placed the literature in a hall drawer and glanced at the mirror. *Gotta clean up before I go. Shit, what can I tell her? Will she understand why I might have to leave? How do I tell her I'm not Hank Malone?*

CHAPTER 16

Long Harbor Police Chief Ted Hanson sat in The Delaware Lounge in the Lenape Casino, formerly Dirty Sam's. He watched patrons hurrying to the gaming floor. *They can't wait to lose their money... Just like me.*

A tall, rugged man in a pale blue shirt and painted tie walked up and pulled out a chair. "Hello, chief. Is this seat taken?"

"Billy Whitedeer, good to see you." Ted looked around and laughed. "Su casa es mi casa."

The casino manager nodded and sat. "I've heard that expression differently, but welcome anyway." He signaled the waitress. "So, what brings you to Lenape, Ted?"

"I'm thinking a little video poker later on. You know, this place is nicer than when it was Dirty Sam's, but it's not as busy."

"Maybe so," Billy said. "But, at least, no one's been killed or shot at, and we haven't been robbed, so this suits me just fine." He looked at Ted's plate. "What are you having?"

"A chef salad with ranch. Evian."

"Seems reasonable. Not like your old boss. As I recall, he was partial to cheesesteaks."

Ted laughed. "Yeah, Mark loved his cholesterol. Not sure how he did it." He stabbed a chunk of ham. "Now he's in Iowa heading up a corporate security firm. He's lost thirty pounds, and is running a few miles every day. Go figure."

A waitress walked up with a menu, but Billy waved it off. "I'll have a cheesesteak with the works, and a large soda." He grinned at Ted. "In honor of former Chief Mark Porfino. May he find a quieter existence in the Hawkeye State as his protégé protects us from harm."

•　　•　　•　　•　　•

Billy returned after filling his Heap Big Lenape Megagulp with Dr. Pepper. Ted studied the plastic cup which had an image of an Indian stalking a buffalo.

"Don't you get tired of the stereotypes, Billy?"

The fifth-generation Lenape Indian analyzed the hunting scene. "Not sure we had buffalo in Jersey back then." He turned to watch a crowd of senior citizens coming through the walkway leading from the transit area. "We have different game now." He laughed. "And just as cunning."

He sat back. "And what game is Chief Hanson hunting these days?"

Ted pushed some ranch onto a slice of turkey, balanced dressing, meat, and lettuce with his fork and slid the mixture into his mouth. He chewed slowly, swallowed, then sipped his Evian.

"Our big task now is monitoring the traffic around the construction of the Town Centre. That's C-E-N-T-R-E, Billy. High-priced consumerism has come to Long Harbor: Louis Vuitton, Gucci, McCormick and Schmick's." He popped a cherry tomato into his mouth, gagged, and then coughed it out. "Anyway, construction is progressing at a good pace."

Billy poured ketchup on his cheesesteak and took a long sensuous bite. Further mastication was undetectable, as his mouth changed shape, grunts emanated, and then an anaconda-like swallow. *Did his jaw just unhinge?* He wiped his mouth, ketchup and cheese DNA staining the napkin. "I read in the paper that the South Jersey mob, among other groups, are trying to grab control on the ground level. Mario Gallante's old crew, and others. Any truth to that?"

Ted leaned toward Billy. "Look, you have a good feel for the community, so I'll let you in on some of the details. Maybe you can keep your eyes and ears open."

He positioned his chair closer. "We're monitoring the comings and goings, as is The Long Harbor Press obviously, and the state police.

Mario isn't directly hands-on anymore, but is still considered to be the puppet master. We don't count him out, but there's a younger, more aggressive set of thugs who are the face of Gallante. Our moles tell us that Town Centre is a high priority in their efforts to grab more control in south Jersey."

Ted took the last sip from the bottle, then placed his spotless napkin on the table. "The Gallante folks don't play well with others. We're watching them closely."

He picked up his napkin and dabbed a wet spot on the table "Also, besides the mob, there's two other strong-armed entities fighting for control in Town Centre. One is the Mormon Mafia."

"You can't be serious."

Ted shook his head. "I wish I was, but they exist. A leadership group moved eastward and recruited heavily. They're involved in construction and real estate. Can be somewhat ruthless from what I hear. They've established a headquarters in Camden."

"And the third set of criminals?"

"Amazon."

CHAPTER 17

Hank sat at a small table at Giorgio's waiting for Sue. He watched townspeople passing by on this early Saturday afternoon. *Man, I'll miss this town if I need to move away. Jersey has an edge. Not like Salt Lake City.*

His favorite waitress, Milly, delivered a Flying Fish. He wiped the moisture from the bottle of extra pale ale and examined the label. Made just a few miles away in Somerdale. *Good coffee, good beer. A little crowded, but a different experience every time you venture out.*

A woman in hospital scrubs walked in, saw Hank, and flashed a Mary Richards smile while doing the character's goofy wave. *It's like she just stepped out of The Mary Tyler Moore Show.* Hank stood, and pulled out the neighboring chair. Sue bounded over, pecked him on the cheek and situated herself on the torn pleather.

Milly appeared out of nowhere and handed her a menu. "A Flying Fish?" she asked. "Or are you on the clock?"

Sue sighed as she examined Hank's glass, the foam slowly dissolving away. "Boy, I need one, but I better not." She handed back the unopened menu. "I'll have an ice tea, I'm on a diet ... and a pulled pork sandwich on a potato roll."

Hank handed Milly the menu. "I'll have the bacon cheeseburger."

Sue tapped Milly's arm as she started to leave. "And extra coleslaw for me."

Turning to Hank, Sue sighed and twitched her nose. He melted.

"So, how's work, Sue? Busy today?"

"The usual Saturday crowd: overnight car crashes, sprained ankles from youth soccer, flirting EMTs, interns slogging through a twenty-four hour shift."

Milly delivered the ice tea. Sue positioned the sugar shaker over the rim and poured. Hank mentally counted to five before the flood of sucrose stopped. Sue stirred the mixture and took a long gulp. "Ah. Just right."

Hank sipped his beer, his slight tremor causing foam to dot his nose. "Sue..."

His girlfriend giggled and grabbed her napkin. "You have beer on your nose. Now sit still while I clean you up."

Hank caught her hand as she wiped and stroked it. This odd romantic gesture ended when Milly arrived carrying the pulled pork and Hank's bacon cheeseburger. The couple disengaged and sat motionless as Milly set down the entrees. "Is there anything else you need?" asked Milly, then feeling the moment, walked away.

●   ●   ●   ●   ●

Sue dug into the coleslaw while studying Hank, who played with a dill pickle. "What's the matter, Hank? You look like you're worried about something."

"I'm not sure I like it here in Long Harbor, Sue. What if I had to move on? Maybe go away real fast?"

Sue dropped her roll, the pork drippings covering her thumbs. "What are you saying, Hank? Are you dumping me?" She wiped her hands in a napkin. "We've been dating for two years." She leaned forward. "Now you do this?"

An elderly couple at the next table stood, check in hand, preparing to leave. The wife focused a lethal glare at Hank, who collected himself. "Just a misunderstanding, folks. Have a nice day."

He turned to Sue, who kept turning a steak knife in her hand. "Baby, I would never leave you. I just wondered how attached you are to Long Harbor. Wouldn't you want to leave this place with me and go somewhere less busy?"

"But why, Hank? You have a good union job and plenty of carpentry work in the Town Centre. And now you're close to becoming a foreman. I'm up for head nurse at Memorial Hospital." She picked up a waffle chip and pointed it at Hank. "We got it good here. Why should we leave?"

Hank took a bite of his burger and chewed, slowly, hoping for inspiration. "Just a wild thought, Sue. If you like it here, we'll stay."

"Now, that's the Hank Malone I know. Feet solidly on the ground. Ready to take on everything life throws at him."

He emptied his remaining beer in one long gulp, and steadied himself. "You're right, Sue. This is where I belong."

CHAPTER 18

Elder Olsen walked into the meetinghouse in Camden, placed his materials into a cubbyhole, and entered his small office. He logged into his laptop, put in earbuds, and recorded his progress for the day: plenty of materials handed out, some promising contacts, and mild interest from a few others.

Ward Leader Steve Yount knocked on the door frame and waited for Olsen to look up. "Come in, Leader Yount," Olsen said after seeing the man's large shadow eclipse his modest desk. Olsen removed his earbuds, muted the *Bleed from Within* video, and sat at attention.

Steve pulled a chair, and gestured to the heavy metal band on Olsen's screen. "Not my cup of tea, Nick, but a break from the Tabernacle Choir, I guess."

Nick laughed, closed the screen, and brought up his notes. "Long Harbor is a tough place to spread the word. They have a casino that either employs them or relieves them of their money. They're into sports, Saturday morning drinking, and large pastries. They also hide pretty well, so it isn't easy to engage them. One man only talked to me through a curtain and hid his face when he saw me, like if we didn't make eye contact, we wouldn't bother with him."

"Well, it's a tough job, Nick, but the rewards are worth it. Spreading God's word isn't easy or profitable." He laughed. "Or everyone would do it."

Nick stood and turned to the window. "Funny thing, this was my first time in that section of Long Harbor, but I swear, even though I didn't catch his full face, I've seen that man before."

"Occupational hazard, Nick. Doing this week in and week out must make everyone looks the same." He walked over and patted Nick on the shoulder. "Maybe you need a break from the door-to-door."

He pulled his wallet and removed a business card. "Leader Cummings is heading up a group of young missionaries like yourself working on the construction of the new Town Centre in Long Harbor. This is a good opportunity for us, Nick. Getting in at the ground level. Being able to strengthen our foothold in New Jersey and establishing a business presence."

Steve picked up the Rubik's Cube from Nick's desk and rotated the sides for a few seconds. "Lucky I don't do this for a living." He huffed. "This is a real bitch. Oops, sorry, challenge from the Lord."

He handed the cube to Nick, who lined the sides in the correct sequence within a minute. "It's not that difficult, Leader Yount. Just practice and patience."

"Good, Nick. Patience, as they say, is a virtue. Do you have any trade skills? Something specific we can use down there?"

"Well, I love carpentry. It's a chance to build something lasting and beautiful from scratch." He laughed. "And, of course, my Lord and Savior was a Jewish carpenter."

Steve laughed. "That one never gets old. I'll call Cummings and let him know you'll meet with him first thing Monday." He handed him the card.

Nick watched from the doorway as Steve left and navigated the corridor to his office. He passed a bulletin board. On the upper left hand corner was a ten-by-twelve picture with a caption, "HAVE YOU SEEN ME?" Above it was a picture of Louie Kimball, a man wanted by the LDS.

CHAPTER 19

Sunday morning. St. Augustine's Roman Catholic Church stood out against the backdrop of factories, farms, and, in the distance, the cleared land for the Town Centre. Sue and Hank walked through the vestibule, nodded to a parish greeter, and sought a pew. Sue blessed herself with holy water and Hank did the same, feeling somewhat blasphemous.

They found a row in the middle, genuflected and scooched in. Sue knelt, made a sign of the cross, and bowed her head in prayer. Hank mimicked his girlfriend's actions and winced as the kneeler dug into his knees. He waited for Sue to finish her conversation with God and sit back. Hank, relieved, did the same.

Sue opened the church bulletin and peered over news of the parish, the sick list, and when the next bus trip to Lenape Casino was occurring. Hank studied the architecture of the church. *Must be a hundred years old. A lot of elaborate detail in the wood and the statues. These Catholics know how to do it up.*

Bells rang out and the congregation stood. Hank steadied himself on the back of the pew in front of him and awaited the priest. Sue and the regulars started singing. She poked Hank with an elbow and pointed to a page in the hymn book: *How Great Thou Art*. Hank hummed along until he caught up to the lyrics chanted by the congregation.

Father Theo walked up the aisle, preceded by altar servers: one boy, one girl. He nodded to Sue and Hank as he made his way to the front. *Boy, if he only knew who I was.*

The mass completed in just under an hour, Hank rubbed his knees after the priest and servers passed by. He and Sue left the pew and were absorbed into a sea of hungry faithful heading to their cars. They took part in a strange automotive dance with the others, emptying the parking lot without undoing the well-intentioned Christianity they'd just experienced. They drove toward Sheila's Diner, the earthly reward for the weekly homage to their creator.

●   ●   ●   ●   ●

Sheila's Diner, the stainless steel framed hub of Long Harbor social life, stood at the ready for the Sunday morning onslaught. Sheila watched the cars full of churchgoers pull into the lot and empty out. "Get ready," she called out. The wait staff stood by, order books in hand.

The couple sandwiched into the waiting area. Hank navigated the perilous steps to the hostess station and gave Sheila his name, which was added to an already long list. He found Sue on his return trip, standing by the bakery counter, examining an enormous bear claw under glass. "Sheila says 20 minutes," he told her.

Sue took a deep breath and emitted a sigh. "I can smell the scrapple and, I'm guessing, Italian sausage."

"Your million dollar schnoz," Hank said, laughing. "Ready to track down diner prey before it can escape."

He pulled his phone and checked the sports news. The Predators, Long Harbor's perennial losing football franchise, had signed a journeyman quarterback, destined to be a trivia question in a few more lackluster years.

He checked his email. Larry Marino, his boss at the Town Centre, topped the list of senders. "Hank: We have two new apprentices starting Monday. I want you to show them the ropes. One is Mike Angeloni, from Gallante Plumbing in Cambria. Another goombah, but don't let that intimidate you, heh, heh. The other is Nick Olsen, from

Smith Enterprises in Camden. He comes highly recommended by Stan Cummings. Both new men will be stopping by your trailer for orientation and assignment. See you Monday. Larry."

Nick Olsen. Could that be the elder who visited Saturday? Smith Enterprises. Damn. Of course, Joseph Smith. How come I never made the connection?

"What's up, Hank. Get bad news?"

Hank put his phone away and sighed. "Nothing I can't handle, Sue. Nothing I can't handle."

CHAPTER 20

Monday morning. Chief Ted Hanson sat in the cruiser, Ned Fuller from the state police in the passenger seat. "People are really dragging in today, Ned. Must have been a good weekend."

"And look at those clouds," Ned said. "Not long before it starts raining." He sipped his coffee, then stuffed most of a crème-filled donut into his mouth. "We have a tough job, but at least we keep dry most of the time."

Ted started to signal the powdered sugar outlining Ned's lips, but stopped when a pickup sped into the lot, its muffler announcing the arrival. The driver pulled next to a construction trailer, sat still for a minute, then climbed out. He leaned against the truck bed and folded his arms.

"That's Hank Malone." Ted said, nodding to the pickup. "Construction supervisor and soon to be foreman of the whole project. A close friend of mine. He must be waiting for someone."

A Ford Explorer pulled up and three men got out. The driver, a large man who hadn't missed many meals, waved to Hank and signaled the men to follow.

"That's Larry Marino, current construction lead and soon to be one of the board members of Town Centre," Ted said.

Larry shook Hank's hand and introduced his passengers. After greetings all around, the man returned to his Explorer, honked once, and drove away.

• • • • •

"Let's go inside, guys. Before it starts raining," Hank said. He climbed the temporary wooden steps, pushed the metal door open and signaled Mike Angeloni and Nick Olsen to enter. Drops started to fall.

"There's coffee on the counter. Got to warn you, it's strong and bitter. There's sugar, and some artificial creamer."

Mike filled a cup, added sugar and slid into a swivel chair. Nick sat. "No coffee for me, Hank," he said. "I never touch the stuff."

Of course, you don't, Olsen. Joseph Smith preached against it.

Hank opened a drawer, pulled out forms and handed each a pen. "Fill these out, men. Be sure to include the make and license of your car. You'll need a permit to park here."

The men worked on the forms as Hank sipped his coffee. He pretended to leaf through paperwork. When Nick got to the automobile information, Hank peered over his shoulder and read. *Crap, the license I saw Saturday. It definitely <u>is</u> the same guy who came to my door. I wonder if he recognizes me.*

CHAPTER 21

Hank sat in the trailer and stared out the dusty window. Town Centre was taking shape. More men and women came on to the job every day, almost exclusively from Smith Industries, Gallante Plumbing, or Amazon.

The Amazons gave Hank the willies. Brought in by Amazon Building Services, they were hipsters with college degrees, led by Maurice Lobo. While focusing on their own brick and mortar bookstore, which had a large footprint in what would soon be Centre Square, they also provided trade skills to other high-end stores. They exuded this quiet confidence, which impressed the other tradesman. Oddly, they seemed even more religious than the Smith people. Amazon must promise some salvation not normally associated with the almighty.

The Smith Industries folks, led by Stan Cummings, were clearly LDS now that Hank thought about it. Neat, clean, men and women. Not a cigarette or thermos of coffee between them. Hank didn't chat with many of them, but wasn't surprised that they were prompt, friendly and efficient. They also exuded a subtle menace that kept the interference of others at a distance.

The Gallante Plumbing crew, headed by Luciano Sancti, were involved in all sections of Town Centre. If you wanted water and sewer, you went through them. They were clearly Italian in origin, and more stereotypical blue-collar types. They told raw jokes, swore, and one of them even whistled at a Smith female. He called in sick the next day and wasn't seen again.

This was Hank's realm, a kingdom of serfs who barely trusted each other and vied for his approval and that of the project partners. He knew he had to tread lightly, not showing favoritism to any group.

•　　•　　•　　•　　•

Hank looked at his watch: 5 p.m. Dinner with Sue tonight. He called La Scala and confirmed his 7 o'clock reservation. *Our second anniversary dating. Why do women get hung up on such things? What about important dates, like July 10, three years ago? Bradshaw and his mob partners were convicted, the FBI whisked me away, handed me papers making me officially Hank Malone, and escorted me to Long Harbor, New Jersey. About as far from the brotherhood that you could get.*

Nick Olsen turned a corner from the *Harry Winston* site and walked toward Hank's trailer. *Now we're crawling with them.* Hank sat, pretended to work on his laptop, and glanced out the window, awaiting his visitor.

Nick stopped, appearing to wait for something. A blue SUV pulled up, and he climbed into the passenger side. The Smith Enterprises logo reflected the late afternoon sunlight.

Hank focused on the driver, an older man. Nick pointed to the foreman's trailer as Hank moved out of the sightline, and peered from a curtain in the corner. For a few uncomfortable seconds, the man stared at the main trailer window, then tapped his watch, saying something to him. The men drove away.

•　　•　　•　　•　　•

Hank returned home, showered, put on clean shirt, tie, and slacks, and studied himself in the mirror. He examined his face. *Had to admit, the surgeon did a good job creating a new jaw line and flattening my nose. I'm a new man.* He tightened his tie. *Sayonara, Louie. Forever.*

He took a velvet box from his bureau drawer, flipped it open, and admired the sparkle that emanated from the diamond. *It's now or never, Hank. Let's make Sue an honest woman.*

•　　•　　•　　•　　•

Hank found a parking spot a half block and across the street from the restaurant. He checked his breath, climbed out of his pickup and started walking to La Scala. He patted his pocket, feeling for the box. He still couldn't believe he had conjured up the guts to propose.

He found the crosswalk and still had to dodge drivers escaping town in the late afternoon. He reached the police headquarters building, newly renovated from wage taxes coming from Town Centre.

At a third-floor window, he saw the chief of police, his best friend, Ted Hanson. Ted was a fellow Predators fan and season ticket holder. He had risen through the ranks, working with former Chief Mark Porfino on some of the more scandalous crimes in this small town: murder, manslaughter, a casino heist. They even matched wits with Leona Galley, the infamous Red Dahlia, florist, and assassin.

Now, with Mark gone, this was Ted's realm. Hank would joke that Ted should loosen up and enjoy this shore town and its amenities. After all the crime sprees of the past ten years, statistically, this small town was due for a prolonged period of nothing more than petty crime. Nothing too serious to uproot the peace and quiet he deserved.

Ted didn't know that Long Harbor was now home to a wanted man. Someone who disguised his appearance to escape his past. Someone who drank with him at football games, and commiserated afterward on their team's lack of defense.

Ted saw Hank and waved. Hank returned the gesture with the Benny Hill backhand salute that never failed to crack his friend up. Ted returned a regulation salute.

Hank walked on. *I love this town. Dammit, I'm staying put.*

•　　•　　•　　•　　•

Like every town in south Jersey, Long Harbor is home to a dozen Italian restaurants. La Scala was rated the best by The Long Harbor Press, the review proudly displayed in the window next to a statue of St. Francis of Assisi.

Hank entered to the sound of Dean Martin crooning *That's Amore*. He started to hum as he walked up to Antony, the host. "Ah, Mr. Malone, we have your table available, in the back, in a cozy corner."

Dean sang about pasta fazool as Antony navigated Hank past a dessert cart and a wine bucket. He stopped at a small table in the corner. "Here you go, Hank. Very romantic."

Hank studied the menu as a glass of Chianti was placed in front of him. "Compliments of Antony," said Mona, his waitress. "Where's Sue today?"

"She should be here in a few minutes. I guess she was hung up at the hospital."

The door opened and Sue rushed in. Joe Dolce was singing *Whatsa Matta You* from the song *Shaddup You Face*. Sue found Hank as he stood and waved. The song finished. His girlfriend shrugged, laughed, and marched across the room, as Antony chased her with a menu.

"Boy, I was half out the door and a massive head wound came in. Blood everywhere. The poor guy must have been hit by a car, maybe even a train. People around him swooned as he bled and vomited. Marcy said she'd take care of the victim and I should meet my special guy. What a nice friend."

She opened the menu. "So, I'm in the mood for a stiff drink and some calamari." She turned the page of the heavy menu. "And maybe veal parm with angel hair pasta."

Hank fidgeted and checked his pocket for the thousandth time. "What are you having, Hank?"

"Sue. We've dated for over two years now and know each other's quirks," he said, pausing. "But there's something you don't know about me."

"Oh, no. Don't tell me you're gay."

Hank laughed as another song started. Al Alberts crooned, 'On the Way to Cape May.' They both hummed, then sang the catch line. Others joined in as Antony made like the conductor. At the end, applause for the brave couple. Sue and Hank raised their glasses. "Salute!" Sue shouted to their audience.

The diners resumed their meals. "So, you were saying, Hank? Do you have a deep secret I don't know about?"

Hank reached into his pocket and removed the ring box. He stumbled to one knee as the wine and the long table cloth made kneeling difficult.

Sue gasped.

"Susan Taylor. Will you do me the honor of marrying Hank Malone? For better or for worse?"

All eyes on them. Sue paused as seeming to weigh the pluses and minuses. She leaned forward and kissed him. "Of course, I will. You goof."

● ● ● ● ●

Antony brought another bottle of wine, on the house. Fellow diners walked up to the table to congratulate the couple and check out the ring. When they finished dinner, Antony called Uber to deposit the couple at their next destination, Hank's house. They could pick up their cars next day when the wine wore off.

When they left the car, they walked hand-in-hand to the door of the rancher. A paper flyer lay on the welcome mat. "We missed you today," it read. "Let us tell you about the Latter-Day Saints."

CHAPTER 22

Hank arrived at the trailer the next day, an hour late. Nick was examining a blueprint and drinking a smoothie. When he saw Hank, he gestured toward the counter. "Mike made coffee. I have to tell you, it smells great."

Hank pointed at Nick's strawberry drink. "That doesn't look too bad, either."

Wiping condensation from the plastic cup, Nick revealed the source. "Can you believe it? McDonald's."

"I don't suppose you got an Egg McMuffin or Hash Browns?" said Hank, sniffing the air. "I haven't had breakfast yet."

"Oversleep, Hank?"

"No, I had a better offer."

Nick blushed and sipped his drink.

"Nick, my friend. I proposed to my girlfriend last night. Nurse Sue Taylor agreed to become my wife."

"Man, that's great, Hank. Have you set a date?" He walked to the sink, rinsed out the cup and dropped it into the recycle can. He leaned against the counter. "I haven't had much luck with women, myself." He frowned. "I think it's my religion, being a Latter-Day Saint. Probably too much for a Jersey girl to handle."

Hank understood. *Poor Guy.* "Don't worry, Nick. Some fine Garden State girl will see Nick Olsen as a whole and be happy to be by his side."

He walked to the counter and poured a cup of coffee. Nick sniffed and sighed. "As for the date," Hank continued, "I'll let Sue figure that out. I'm guessing the fall, but who knows."

Nick took a plastic card from his pocket and studied it. "Prime football season, Hank. No Saturday games, but you might miss the game the next day." He handed the schedule to Hank.

"Well, we can't do it during Dallas week, that's for sure. November 10th is out."

Hank added sugar to his brew. "Sue is a Jets fan, of all things. I'll need to convert her."

"The Predators are playing the Jets in the first preseason home game. Hank. Maybe you can make her a believer then."

Hank checked the date. Early August. "That's when Phil and his wife go upstate on vacation, and Herb goes to Ocean City, Maryland. Hmmm. That leaves two extra tickets for you and Sue. Join us."

Nick smiled. "Perfect, Hank. It gets lonely sometimes here in Long Harbor. Plus, this will give me a chance to meet your fiancé." He took back the season schedule. "I guess Ted Hanson has already met Sue."

"He has. He keeps saying she's too good for me."

"Hah. She must be quite a lady, then. I look forward to meeting her."

Nick finished his drink. "By the way, my Ward Leader in Camden, Steve Yount, picked me up after work yesterday. We were going to an assembly. I wanted him to meet you, but he said we were late."

Hank dropped the sugar packet into his coffee, then fished it out with a stirrer. "Maybe some other time, Nick"

Boy, last thing I need now is to meet someone from the hierarchy.

CHAPTER 23

Word spread that Hank was getting married. His popularity among the workforce was clear, as calls of congratulations came in, clogging the phone lines. Gallante Plumbing sent an enormous box of candy, and an offer of free plumbing for a year. The Amazons, not to be outdone, sent a $100 gift card, and a Norwegian foot massager. Smith Enterprises sent a Barcalounger. It was good to be king.

Sue moved into Hank's home and quickly undid Hank's hard-earned disorder. In a month she turned the squalor into something from House Beautiful, while also appropriating the foot massager. They agreed to share the lounger.

She jumped at the chance to see her beloved Jets, even in the preseason. As the game approached, she readied her jersey, bought green greasepaint, and practiced her cheers. Some involved a surprising profanity. Sue was no novice in this process. Hank wondered if he could convert her after all.

•   •   •   •   •

Game night. Hank came home from work and raced to his bedroom to change into Predator gear: a Number 10 jersey with "Wilson" stitched on the back, a throwback helmet without a chin strap, and black eye grease. He checked himself in the mirror. *Ready for battle.*

The front door closed with a thud, strong enough to vibrate the frame of the rancher. Heavy footsteps down the hall. Sue appeared, nodded to Hank and removed her nurse's uniform in seconds. Hank was a little turned on, but Sue disappeared into the bathroom before he could respond.

A flush followed by faucets turning and then gargling. Sue returned, stark naked, and stopped suddenly. She caught Hank staring. "What? Is there something you haven't seen before?"

Hank tried to look at her eyes.

"Forget it, Hank. Gotta get ready for the game. Carpe diem."

Hank turned pale. *That expression again.*

"What's up, Hank. You look like you've seen a ghost." No response. "Now if you wouldn't mind leaving the room, I need to get ready for our evening out."

Hank walked back down the hall and sat in the Barcalounger. Picking up the remote, he found ESPN and tried to concentrate on the sports chatter. *Carpe freakin' diem. Boy, that brings everything back.*

Minutes later, his intended walked into the living room and twirled 360 degrees. "What do you think, Hank?" she said. "Am I ready for battle?"

He took inventory: green Number 12 jersey with "Barlow" on the back, skin-tight white pants with a green stripe running the length, green eye grease with "Barlow" stenciled in white, green sneakers.

"Seems like you have everything you need."

"Go J-E-T-S, Jets," she shouted. "Beat those freakin' Predators."

"Now you're ready."

•　　•　　•　　•　　•

Hank and Sue joined the crush of humanity walking to the stadium from the parking lots, mostly Predators jerseys with the smattering of Jets gear. New York was 100 miles away, so hearing fans with distinct accents and attitudes wasn't unexpected. *At least, they're not Giant fans.*

Sue nodded to each Jet compatriot, at least those not drunk enough to know where they were. Ted spotted the couple and hurried over. Nick Olsen appeared from the crowd and joined them. The two men took a moment to study Sue's getup and signaled their approval.

Hank put his arm on Nick's shoulder. "Sue, this is Nick Olsen from my crew at Town Centre."

Sue extended her hand. "Glad to meet you, Nick. Hank talks a lot about you, his carpentry apprentice. I sometimes think he sees a younger version of himself in you."

Hank coughed.

"I hope you're keeping my fiancé honest down at the site," Sue continued.

"Sue, Hank is as honest as you can get. You don't have to worry about him."

Sue pointed to the clock outside the stadium. "A half hour till game time, Gents. I need a beer and something greasy." She raised her arms and made a whooshing sound. "So, why are we gassing out here, when there's Predator butt to be kicked?"

Hank, Ted, and Nick glanced around. No glares from those passing by. A preseason game doesn't bring the same intensity or madness as the regular season. The men laughed. "This way, Sue," Hank said. "Ladies, children, and Jet fans first."

•　　•　　•　　•　　•

The four found their end zone seats. Sue left with Ted for food, while Hank and Nick watched the players stretching and kickers and punters loosening up their legs. The Predator mascot — Diver, a Turkey vulture — taunted the Jets players. The Jets punter approached from behind and stepped on Diver's foot, causing a pratfall enjoyed by his teammates.

Pushing and shoving ensued among players and mascots of both teams. No melee, though. Frankly, it was well known that the Predator players were creeped out by Diver, who in the offseason had replaced Freedom, a soaring Eagle. No reason to get injured defending an ugly bird.

Sue and Ted returned balancing cardboard food trays. Sue handed a large Pilsner and an enormous sausage sandwich to Hank and kept a Budweiser and cheesesteak for herself. Ted handed Nick a bottle of water and a box of fried chicken. He held on to a Heineken, pulled a pork sandwich, and waved off money from Nick.

Ted leaned forward and squinted. "Hey, Diver is missing his tail."

"He pissed off the wrong Jet," Hank said. "Kickers aren't wrapped too tight."

Sue laughed, then looked at Nick. "So, I'm curious. How'd you get into the construction business?"

Nick thought this over as cheerleaders and the maintenance crew picked up feathers.

"I'm a Latter-Day Saints missionary, knocking on doors and preaching the word of God." He waited for a reaction and got none. "Anyway, my leader asked me if I wanted to work in Town Centre." He laughed. "Get away from the growling dogs, staring kids, and grouchy seniors." He shook his head. "Some of them bite."

"The dogs?"

"All three."

Hank, Sue, and Ted laughed, then dove into their food and drink. Nick positioned his dinner on his lap, spread his hands and mouthed something. He then started eating as his friends watched. "Sorry, a pre-meal prayer," Nick said. "We in the LDS thank God for his bounty."

"We Catholics have a prayer before meals too, but skip it more often than not," Sue said, nudging Hank. "Hank even seems to forget the words. Hard to believe he was raised Catholic."

They didn't teach me to pray in witness protection school. "I know the words," Hank said.

His friends waited. Hank sighed, folded his hands, and lowered his head. "Over the lips and past the gums, watch out stomach, here it comes."

"Amen," said Ted. "Let's eat."

●   ●   ●   ●   ●

The Predators and Jets played to a 13-13 tie. The starters were pulled after one quarter, and the second and third stringers fought it out the rest of the way. By the final gun, only a few thousand fans remained.

Hank, Sue, Ted, and Nick walked the labyrinth of exit ramps until they got to ground level. Ted suggested a stop at Flannigan's, a local watering hole for postgame revelers.

It was clear that the fans who left early went straight to Flannigan's. The four edged into the restaurant area, and because of Ted's popularity with the management, were shown to a table within minutes. They agreed on a pitcher of beer and plates of the hottest wings on the menu. Nick opted for a Sprite, not quite throwing caution to the wind, but an upgrade from bottled water.

The wings arrived, and everyone dove in. Nick didn't yield his ground, working through each piece of chicken like a quarterback carving up a bad secondary. The hot sauce was no match. While the others broke out in sweat, Nick seemed to grow more intense as the orange, greasy mixture formed around his mouth.

Hank threw a half-eaten wing onto his plate. "I'm done." He drained his mug of beer. "I'll pay the price for this tomorrow morning."

Ted also gave up. "I'm done. Damn good, but I think I burned a hole in my esophagus."

"Wimps," said Sue as she matched Nick bone for bone. "Olsen is the only real wing eater in here." She wiped her mouth. "Where'd you get your chicken experience, Nick? I haven't seen anything like that outside of Philly."

Nick took a swig of his Sprite and, using a napkin, discretely removed a sliver of chicken from his incisors. "There wasn't much to do socially in seminary, Sue. A night out in town was usually plates of wings and brisket."

He turned to Hank. "Ever been in Salt Lake City, Hank? A beautiful place."

Hank turned pale and was quiet for a few seconds. "Can't say I have, Nick. Southern Utah for the national parks, but nothing north of Canyonlands."

"You and Sue have to go there sometimes. It's a beautiful place and lots of history to experience." He took another sip of his soda. "I miss it sometimes."

Ted took a swig of his beer and eyed him. "So, Nick, I never asked. How did you end up in New Jersey? Seems a long way from Utah."

"We seek to spread the word across the world. I could have ended up in some far corner of the earth, but instead was assigned to South Jersey." He laughed. "It didn't hurt that my uncle comes from Jersey. He has connections within the hierarchy. He pulled some strings, and here I am."

Ted nodded. "We all need our connections. My stepfather was friends with the police commissioner. Convinced him to take in a raw recruit."

Hank patted Ted on the shoulder. "My friend here is too modest, Nick. He worked his way through the ranks, helped solve multiple capital crimes, and has the skill to schmooze the Long Harbor movers and shakers. He's a friend and a good man to know."

"And your boss here, Nick," Ted said, gesturing to Hank. "A straight shooter if there ever was one. He showed up in town three years ago and immediately settled in." He pointed to Sue. "And had the good sense to meet and date the funny, kind, and industrious Sue Taylor, soon to be head nurse at Memorial Hospital."

Nick sighed. "I have to admit I'm unlucky in love. I think my religion is a real turnoff for women. They seem to think I'm some sort of monk, clean living and unapproachable. Well, I have my human side. I like a good time like anyone else."

Hank raised his glass and gestured his friends to follow. "Here's to Nick Olsen. Fine young man, wing eater extraordinaire, and overall good guy. A valued asset to Long Harbor and Town Centre."

• • • • •

Hank and Sue reached home about 2 a.m. Sue was feeling amorous and removed all clothing except for her jersey. She walked out of the bathroom expecting to ravish Hank. Her fiancé was unconscious on his side of the bed, snoring and passing wind.

Sue held her breath and walked to the living room. She found her address book and leafed through the pages. "Gina Mancini," she mumbled. "Now, *she* would make a nice match for Nick Olsen."

CHAPTER 24

Monday morning. Hank entered the trailer and examined the duty report. Nick had already signed in thirty minutes earlier and was over at the Harry Winston site working with his team on the framing. It was a tricky build because a vault needed to be installed to protect the jewelry.

The Amazons were signed in as well. Maurice Lobo ran a tight ship, putting his crew through fifteen minutes of calisthenics every morning, then they meditated for five minutes. None of this was on the clock, so Hank didn't object. Still, seemed even more religious than the LDS, who took care of their daily connection to the almighty before entering the site.

The goombahs from Gallante Plumbing, though mostly Catholic, were present and accounted for. Unlike their peers, they showed no outward devotion to higher powers, unless swearing could be considered a form of prayer.

Still, these three groups maintained a professional, if not cordial, relationship, so far. There were occasional sharp words, and one time a fistfight, but overall, a working detente.

Hank took a sip of coffee and peered out the window. There was Ted sitting in his cruiser, eating a donut and watching the comings and goings. *What does he think will happen?*

●   ●   ●   ●   ●

Hank met Nick for lunch at the trailer. The pizza arrived just in time. "I don't know how guys can brown bag it at work. Who wants a warm, soggy sandwich when you can be chowing down on pepperoni, mushrooms, and cheesy bread?" Hank said, catching a string of cheese before it attached to his work shirt.

Nick bit into a slice of mushroom. "MMMM," said Nick. He held up his index finger, the universal sign of something to say after swallowing. He chased down the sauce-soaked slice with a gulp of 7 Up, then sat back. "This *is* darn good, Hank. Jersey has it all over Salt Lake City when it comes to Italian."

Hank laughed. "I'm glad to hear that, Nick," he said, dabbing his chin. "The Italian women here are also something to appreciate." He put down his slice and sat back. "Sue and I were talking on Saturday and she wants to introduce you to her friend, Gina. She's a nurse at Memorial Hospital, like Sue." Hank took a sip of his Dr. Pepper. "Pretty easy on the eyes, too, as I recall."

His friend sat in silence, picking garlic powder off his cheesy bread.

"Now there's no pressure, here, Nick. Just two friends coming to our house for dinner and cards. Next Saturday, if that's good with you."

"OK, Hank. That sounds good." He wiped grease from his fingers. "Does Sue's friend know my religious background? That can be a bit of a turn-off."

"We all have things that set us apart, Nick." He leaned in closer. "Gina is a Giants fan, for example. No accounting for belief systems. So, among a Catholic Predators fan, a Jets fan, a Mormon, and a Lutheran Giants fan, we should have a lot to talk about."

Hank stared at the oil-stained pizza box. "Now, Nick, for the *big* question. Can I have that last slice?"

•　　•　　•　　•　　•

Hank returned home that evening, found the Barcalounger and leafed through the Long Harbor Press. Sue pounced from nowhere, positioned herself on the ottoman and pulled the paper from his hands. "So, did you ask him, Hank? Is he coming to dinner on Saturday?"

"He is. And looks forward to meeting Gina. I told him, no pressure, just friends having dinner."

"Great. What happens, happens." Sue emitted that smirk that indicated she was one step further into her plan.

"Did you know that you look like Snidely Whiplash when you're cooking something up? All you need is a handlebar mustache."

"Well, don't worry, I won't tie Nick to the railroad tracks, Dudley Do-Right." She grinned. "Although the thought of Gina coming to his aid and saving him does have a romantic twist to it."

•　　　•　　　•　　　•　　　•

Saturday evening. Nick rang the doorbell a few minutes after seven, holding a large bottle of Chianti. Hank answered, holding a spatula, and wearing an apron reading "Kiss the Cook." "Nick, come in. Welcome to our humble abode."

Nick stepped in after wiping his shoes on the mat. "This house seems familiar." He laughed. "I guess I saw so many they all look alike."

Hank fumbled the spatula.

Nick inhaled. "I smell garlic bread, and ... if I'm not mistaken, Bruschetta," he said, waving his hand in front of his nose to gather in the fragrance.

"Guilty as charged, Mr. Olsen," Hank said, laughing. "I don't have an ounce of Italian blood in me, but I developed a soft spot for cooking when I was a bachelor."

"And *eating* his cooking," Sue said, fastening an earring and pecking Hank on the cheek. She saw the bottle Nick was holding like a football. "Is that Chianti, Nick?" she said. "A perfect choice for our Tuscan evening." She took the bottle, whipped out an opener from seemingly nowhere, and had it open in seconds. "We have to give it time to breathe."

A knock on the open door. A tall, well-proportioned brunette in high heels, holding a tray of empty pastry shells, smiled at Sue as the hostess greeted her. "Gina, Just in time. Come in." Sue took the tray.

The woman raised her index finger. "I'll be right back, Sue. Have to make two trips." She returned in a minute holding a clear plastic bag filled with a white cream. "Cannoli filling. You can only fill the shell when ready to eat. Keeps them from getting soggy."

She turned to the men and nudged Hank, who winced from the sharp elbow, then realized he was neglecting his social duty. "Gina, this is Nick Olsen, a carpenter at Town Centre, football fan, and overall good guy," he said.

She stepped forward and offered her hand. "Pleased to meet you. Sue was telling me about you."

Nick shook her hand, his clammy palm enveloping her soft but dry counterpart. He was silent, but then turned to the Chianti. "I brought wine. Looks like we have the complete Italian meal."

"Oh, wait a minute," Gina said. She reached into her coat pocket and removed a baggie filled with chocolate chips. "The cannolis are naked without these."

•　　•　　•　　•　　•

The dinner went well. Bruschetta, spaghetti, sausage, salad, garlic bread, wine, cannolis, and conversation. Gina bemoaned the Giants' lack of offense, Sue talked of the Jets' young quarterback, and Hank laid out the Predators' defensive challenges. This left Nick, who wiped his mouth and thought it over. "No favorite pro team, I guess," he said. "Though I was a big fan of BYU when I was in college."

Gina took a sip of wine. "Sue mentioned that you were from Utah. Wonderful country out there. Our family went on vacation out west when I was ten. Utah stood out for its sheer physical beauty."

"Did you get to Salt Lake City?" Nick asked.

"We did. Dad just had to reaffirm his ancestry. I mean, we're so Italian we bleed tomato gravy, yet he had to check in the Family History Library. Once they confirmed our Mediterranean genealogy, Pop left the building, chest pumped out, ready to sing *O Sole Mio* in the middle of Temple Square."

Nick poured the remaining Chianti for Gina, Hank, and Sue. "My ancestors came from all over Europe. Embarrassing to say that I never delved deeply into the pre-U.S. years. The Olsens *did* make the trek from Illinois to Utah in 1846. A rough passage through unfriendly territory. My brethren survived and settled in The Great Salt Lake City."

Hank was getting anxious. A little too close to home. He stood and raised his glass. "To friends, wherever they come from. May we all live in peace in South Jersey."

"That's an odd toast, Hank," Sue said. "Sounds so dismissive of the past. We should embrace it, warts and all. It defines us as surely as the present." She shrugged. "I always thought we are now what we were before. Some changes in appearance maybe, but the same person deep down inside."

Draining the last sip of the wine, Hank sat and thought this over. *Am I the same? Will Louie Kimball come out one day when I least expect it?*

Sue put her hand on Hank's arm, breaking him from his trance, He flinched. "What's wrong, Hank? It's like you've seen a ghost."

He saw the concern in his friends. "It must be the wine." He poured some water for himself. "What's the Italian expression? In vino, veritas?"

"In wine, there is truth," Gina said. "Don't worry, Hank. There's enough ancient history to go around. While we remember the past, it's best to live in the here and now. The past is over." She raised her glass. "To the present and future. To what we can see in front of us, and to what lies ahead unknown."

"Amen," said Nick. He stood and raised his glass of water. "To friends and acquaintances, past, present, and future." He laughed. "And to quote my uncle, 'May we see them before they see us.'"

CHAPTER 25

Mario Gallante strutted into Lenape Casino. Billy Whitedeer stopped short and sat outside the Starbucks, blending in and watching the mob boss. Mario walked to the Delaware Lounge and studied the menu as he stood in line. When he reached the counter, he chatted up the hostess, and pointed to the sandwich menu. He held his hands about a foot apart, presumably to indicate the size of his meal.

Mike Angeloni entered minutes later, Billy taking note but not sure why. Just something about the guy. The young man stopped and studied the neon-lit directory. He moved his finger down the listings and focused on the restaurant section. He walked in the direction of the Delaware Lounge.

The mob boss motioned his employee over. They spoke briefly, and the big man pointed to the counter, apparently telling Mike to order. Mario found a table, raised his head when his name was called over the microphone, and beckoned the server to deliver his meal: an enormous cheesesteak and a trough of fries. He smothered the steak and fries with ketchup and took a bite. Ecstasy, clear to Billy from his vantage point.

Billy walked over and sat two tables away in the mostly empty restaurant. He took out his cell and swiped randomly, hoping to seem like any other consumer addicted to his smartphone.

Mike walked to the table, opened his bottled water, and sat. Mario kept eating. A young server, wearing a headband with cardboard feathers, wandered among the rows of tables. "Mike A?" he called out.

Mike signaled him over. The teen placed the meal on the table, opposite Mario. The mob boss squinted and examined the tray: minestrone and avocado chips. He shook his head. "That's not a meal, Mike. That's what you feed animals that become your meal."

Billy smiled to himself. I hear you loud and clear, Mario, he thought. Keep talking.

Mario took another bite and wiped his smeared face with a fistful of napkins. "So, Mike, how's it going at Town Centre? I can't stay long. Technically, I'm not allowed in the casino, but I think I can grab a sandwich without security stopping by."

"OK, I guess, Mario." He turned his head, checking for anyone near. Billy ducked to avoid eye contact, crouched closer to his phone, and swiped madly. Mike leaned closer to the mob boss. "This is a little open, but besides the tech head playing with his phone, we're alone."

He crunched on an avocado chip. "All quiet there. We're scoping out points of weakness in the construction crew — seeing how we can edge closer to controlling the infrastructure. Malone has everything pretty much in control, though. And I don't think he can be bought off."

"Everyone has a price, or a history, Mike," Mario said, dangling a fried onion over his mouth and dropping it in. "We just have to figure out what that is. In the meantime, be a fine young soldier for your boss, Luciano. Have your friends cause just enough discomfort to keep any distrust active, just don't let things boil over for now. There's time for that later on."

He pointed to Mike's plate. "Now, finish up your meal and get back to the Centre. You're doing a good job. Sometime soon our efforts will pay off."

When the men left, Billy dialed Ted Hanson. "Ted, Billy here. I just saw Mario Gallante talking to a 'Mike A' about Town Centre. He must be one of the Gallante crew. Sounded like they were cooking something up to muscle further into control, didn't give a time frame."

"Thanks, Billy," Ted said. "Now we have a name we can track. And soon a face, I hope. This helps a lot."

• • • • •

Hank finished his lunch and stood outside the trailer, leaning on the wooden railing and observing the workmen as they returned. Town Centre was transforming from a dust-driven mixture of heavy equipment and construction sounds to a city of storefronts. The bright colors and logos announcing future occupants covered the walls enclosing the work still underway.

Ted Hanson and the police no longer patrolled traffic flow in the mornings, although a cruiser would drive by once in a while. This little mixture of South Jersey Italians, Latter-Day Saints, and Amazonians seemed to be functioning without major upheaval ... so far. The occasional strong words and pushing and shoving were notable only by their infrequency. Hank was governing his own little United Nations.

CHAPTER 26

Wedding day approached. Sue was given her bachelorette party at Muscle Beach, a male revue club outside the city limits. She swore to Hank afterward that she was a perfect lady. A hard sell when she pulled a G-string from her coat pocket. "Now, how did that get there?"

"Don't ask, don't tell," Hank responded.

"Ted's in charge of my bachelor party. He chose the Birds of a Feather gentleman's club. Not an easy choice, I guess, as his wife, Rhonda, was formerly a star attraction. He told me that not only didn't she object, but, in fact, called her ex-colleagues and asked them to make my night *special,* without crossing any line over which I might not return."

●　　　●　　　●　　　●　　　●

Ted, Hank, Nick, Luciano Sancti, and Maurice Lobo walked into the dark and surprisingly chilly club. Ted had reserved a table near the stage. Pitchers of beer and baskets of chicken wings were placed on the table by smiling, G-string clad women.

"Hi, I'm Lucretia," said a hostess. "I'll be your personal guide to Birds of a Feather. She stood back and looked at each man carefully. "Now, who's the guest of honor?"

Hank raised his hand slowly. Maurice grabbed his elbow and raised it high. Ted opened a paper bag and brought over a crown adorned with plastic chicken parts, metal beer cans, and a groom without pants. "This is Hank, Lucretia. Be gentle with him."

She straddled herself on his lap and whispered in his ear as she buried Hank's face into her cleavage. Hank managed to lift his face from his silicon prison. "Is what you said even legal, Lucretia?"

"In most states, Hank. Though maybe not in the Bible Belt."

Hank took a breath, waited for all body parts to return to normal, and shook his head. "I think I'll pass on that, though I'll always remember the offer."

She feigned disappointment. "I'll give you a rain check, Hank. Someday when you're feeling lonely."

Boy, I've heard that before.

Lucretia removed herself from Hank's lap and adjusted her outfit "So, gentlemen, enjoy the entertainment, and signal for more food and drink when you want. The night is young."

●　　●　　●　　●　　●

Hank returned about 3 a.m. Sue awoke and turned to her fiancé who had been trying to undress without waking her. "So, how was it, Hank? Did Birds of a Feather match its reputation?"

"It did." He removed his pants. "Rest assured I was a perfect gentleman."

Sue squinted. "Wait a minute, Hank. What's that in your left pocket?"

Hank reached inside and pulled out a pink thong. "Ted!" he exclaimed. "I should have suspected that."

"So, you're telling me that the chief of police planted evidence."

"That's my story, Sue. Though I have to admit, part of the night was a blur."

"Don't worry about it, Hank. Just hang the thong next to the underwear I found after my visit to Muscle Beach." She laughed. "Who knows, could be a garment thief in town."

•   •   •   •   •

Hank picked out his tux from the crowded men's store. He chose traditional black with a light green tie to match the bridesmaid dresses. Ted, Luciano, Maurice, and Nick did the same. Nick was flattered that Hank had selected him as a groomsman, their friendship escalating with each day.

Sue's parents, Nancy and Walter, prepared the wedding announcement. They arranged for the couple to pose for photos, then met with them to select the best image. Sue and Hank seemed to agree on a picture, but Hank asked for time to think the whole announcement process over. "I'm just a small town guy. I don't want all this publicity," he said. *Nor a photo of the new Louie in black and white.*

This upset Nancy. Walter understood Hank's reluctance, though not the exact reason. He took him aside. "Hank. Nancy is super excited about the wedding. Give her this. It will make points for you later down the line." Hank nodded and agreed to think it over.

Later that day, Hank called his FBI contact, Charlie Benner. "Hank, no news from you in months. How's wonderful Long Harbor?" He whispered. "Is everything OK?"

"Charlie, I'm getting married next month. Remember I told you about Sue?" He laughed. "Sorry I couldn't invite you to the reception."

"Understood, Hank. I am only a casual acquaintance, after all."

"Well, here's the thing. Sue's parents want to make a wedding announcement in the Long Harbor Press. Picture and all. What do you think?"

Silence. "Boy, that's a tough one, Hank. Let me get back to you. When do you need an answer?"

"Quick, Charlie. Sue's mom is raring to go."

"How bad is the picture?"

"Full frontal." A sigh on the line. Hank sat back and examined the proofs. "You know, there's one where I'm facing the side, looking at Sue. It's the least favorite of all our pictures, but shows only a small part of my face."

"OK, Hank. Sounds like the best choice, I guess. See if you can convince your intended and her parents that this is the picture you want." Charlie's drumming fingers pulsed through the phone. "When will it appear in the paper?"

"They're aiming for the 19th, two weeks before the wedding."

"OK." He sighed. "My best wishes to you, your fiancé and family. Maybe this will just float by unnoticed."

●   ●   ●   ●   ●

On the morning of the 19th, Nancy retrieved the wet and thorn-ridden Long Harbor Press from the rose bush. "I'm gonna give that paperboy a talking to, Walter. I just hope the announcements section isn't soaked."

She flipped to the Local News section. "Thank God, this section is dry." The wedding announcements were at the bottom of the last inside page. "Taylor-Malone. Here it is." She read over the wording which she had previously dictated to the newsroom intern. "Well, he got everything right. I have to give him that."

Walter read over her shoulder and grunted his agreement. They both examined the picture. "That's a lovely picture of the couple," Walter said.

Nancy smiled. "It *is* nice. My family and friends will be so jealous."

"I think you mean pleased, Nancy," Walter said.

"Isn't that what I said?" Nancy replied, studying the groom. "You know, Walt, I hate to say this but from that angle, he looks a little bit like ..."

"Sue's pet from when she was a kid?" Walter asked. "Oh well. We all have our flaws."

●   ●   ●   ●   ●

Hank waited for the paper to arrive. He caught it midair, getting a cheer from the paperboy. He quickly found the announcement: Taylor-Malone. He read the wording, afraid to glance at the picture.

OK, Hank, let's do this. He sat on the porch swing and focused on the photo. *What a relief. It barely shows my face.*

His phone rang. Charlie Benner. "Have you seen the picture, Hank?"

Hank laughed, his relief clear over the connection. "I did, Charlie. Most of my face is hidden."

"OK, Hank. Let's just keep future pictures to a minimum."

"Copy that, Charlie. Boy, that's a load off."

• • • • •

Charlie hung up and studied the picture again. "Shit," he whispered. Sipping his coffee, he pulled a magnifying glass and looked over Hank's picture from different angles.

He found the number for Agent Nelson from the Salt Lake City office. Taking another bite from his coffee roll, he sighed and pressed the dialer. A few rings. Charlie started to disconnect.

"Hello, Mike Nelson here."

Charlie sat in silence.

"Hello, who is this?

"Mike, Charlie Benner from the Philadelphia office. Our mutual client is getting married. His picture is in the local paper."

Silence. "Don't worry, a side angle," Charlie said, clearing his throat. "Our friend is nervous but wants to press on. He has too much at stake now in his life. Wants to keep his roots in South Jersey and raise a family."

"Most of his associates are still in jail, Charlie," Nelson said. "Just one player is out. Carlos Garcia. He's on parole and can't leave Utah for the next two years. He might recognize our client, but I'm sure he doesn't read Jersey papers."

"OK, Mike. I'm going to sit tight and let things develop. Hopefully, this will blow over without fanfare. Our friend is a low profile guy. Maybe he'll fade into the scenery."

CHAPTER 27

Nancy, Walter, Sue, and Hank read the invitations: Hank Malone, of Lawrence, Kansas, was marrying Sue Taylor, of Long Harbor, New Jersey. No mention of Hanks's parents. Both deceased, he explained to them. Died in a tornado.

Kansas was Charlie Benner's brainchild. Charlie attended Kansas University, and was a big fan of *The Wizard of Oz*. The tornado seemed melodramatic, but was accepted by all as a sad setback to Hank's development.

The invitee list was prepared. Sue and Hank insisted on a small wedding, so that made things easier for Hank. No FBI stand-ins needed. No Uncle Sidney, the party animal from Philly. Bureau Chief Sid Baker of the Philadelphia Regional Office was disappointed. He did a good Uncle Sidney.

The invitations went out, a hundred folks, just the right size. About half were Sue's family, the other half mutual friends or work associates. The time leading up to the wedding sped by. Hank consumed by the rapid development of Town Centre, and Sue immersed in her new role of head nurse at Memorial Hospital.

The wedding rehearsal was scheduled for the Thursday before the wedding. Father Theo would lead the wedding party through the steps of the Mass and ceremony. No High Mass. That would have been hard to sit through for pseudo-Catholic Hank. Still, there was enough detail to get down to make him anxious.

Father Theo took Hank aside. "There's no need to be nervous, Hank. Just like Sunday Mass, except we marry you guys at the end." He laughed. "And no mad rush for Sheila's Diner afterward."

Hank pulled a handkerchief and patted his forehead. "Man, I could use a drink."

Father Theo gestured toward Sue, her family, and her attendants congregating in the back. "You're marrying a good woman, Hank. Just relax. It will all be OK."

He patted Hank on the shoulder. "I'll be in the rectory all of tomorrow afternoon. If you feel you need to confess anything, stop in."

Hank laughed. *Boy, if you only knew, Father. I have some doozies that would make your head spin.*

Father frowned at Hank's reaction. "We must all examine our consciences before such big steps, Hank. I hope you're ready to undertake this with a clear knowledge of what marriage means. You and Sue will soon be one. No selfishness, no deep secrets. It's a time for truth."

Hank shook his head. "What are those words Pilate said before washing his hands, Father?" he asked. "The Truth. What is that?"

The priest studied the groom-to-be. "You know, Hank, sometimes you're a real mystery."

●　　　●　　　●　　　●　　　●

Saturday morning. The wedding day. Sue spent her last night as a single woman at Walter's and Nancy's place, her parents insisting on this gesture. The bride can't be seen leaving the groom's home the morning before the ceremony. What would people say?

Hank rose from his restless sleep, started the Keurig, and retrieved Eggos from the freezer. He brushed off the icicles and dropped a pair into the toaster. He picked up the remote and flipped on the local news. A story on Town Centre. Film footage showed the progress made in a little over two years. Hank was seen at a distance, walking with Nick and Maurice. The three men stopped and turned. Hank swiveled away as Nick and Maurice seemed to say something to each other and point to the camera.

The toaster sprang, announcing the readiness of the waffles to be covered in syrup and consumed. Hank almost dropped his coffee at the noise, his attention turning away from the flat screen. *Three years of anonymity, and all of a sudden, I'm smiling in the papers and appearing on camera. What else can happen?*

•　　•　　•　　•　　•

The doors to St. Augustine's Church were open, allowing sunlight to fill the nave and altar with natural light. The flowers were in place, their fragrance wafting throughout. Fans swirled, moving the Indian summer air.

Father Theo dealt, the pile of chips in front of him a testament to his poker skills. It was his idea to play cards to distract Hank from his visible anxiety. Hank, Ted, and Nick checked their cards. Nick's head disappeared under the table. He reemerged with one of his boots and tossed it into the middle. "I'm short on cash. I'll open with a Timberland."

The men laughed. Father Theo undid his belt. "I'll call you with a Montana Silversmith." Hank undid his suspenders and tossed them in. Maurice followed with his cufflinks and vest.

Walter walked in. "The bride has arrived, gentlemen." He noticed the apparel laying on the game table. "Is this some kind of weird strip poker?" he asked. The men laughed.

"No, Walter," Father Theo said. "Just loosening up before the ceremony."

Walter pulled a flask, undid the cap, and took a long pull. "Gentlemen, this is how we unwound in the Marines." He placed the whiskey on the table. "Whet your whistles and let's meet the enemy. I got the wiry woman in the mother-of-the-bride's dress."

•　　•　　•　　•　　•

"If anyone here knows why this couple should not be wed, let him speak now or forever hold his peace." Silence. Hank cringed at first, then straightened up when Sue nudged him. "It's OK, Hank. Just part of the ceremony."

"Going once … going twice," said Father Theo, his lapel microphone reaching the depths of the church. Chuckles in the crowd.

"Then we're good." He raised his hands over the couple. "I now pronounce you man and wife."

Hank pulled Sue into his arms and kissed her so hard she almost fell backward. The maid of honor supported her left shoulder, while Father Theo reached for the right. "Needless to say," he said, "You may kiss the bride."

The couple left the altar and walked down the aisle to applause from the assembled. Smiles to the couple and Nancy and Walter, from family, and friends, and, in the back, Charlie Benner. He gave a thumbs-up to Hank.

●　　●　　●　　●　　●

Hank and Sue stopped at the back, just inside the large wooden doors. Joined by Walter and Nancy and the wedding party, they greeted the well-wishers as they left the church and assembled on the wide stone and concrete steps. The couple stepped out and the crowd unleashed red, blue, and gold balloons. Pictures were taken as the couple stood close together and posed. Walter and Nancy beamed in the background.

After a few minutes, Walter stepped forward. "And now, everyone, the reception is in the parish hall to your left. Let's celebrate this couple." He leaned into Father Theo. "And get a stiff drink." The crowd laughed as the priest motioned to his microphone. "Or, maybe two," he said to his guests.

Hank scanned the crowd. No Charlie Benner. In the distance, he saw his handler's Toyota pulling out of the church parking lot. Stopping at the red light, Charlie glanced over and made eye contact with his charge The light turned green and he drove away.

●　　●　　●　　●　　●

Ted circled the fountain. "Wow, these are the biggest shrimp I've ever seen."

Billy Whitedeer added a few more to his overflowing plate. "They're bigger than anything we have at the casino. The Taylors must have put out lots of money for this." He pointed to a small cocktail table. The men sat on the raised chairs and swiveled.

"Oh, boy," Ted said. "I could use this in my office. Sometimes, I have to keep close track of those knuckleheads."

Billy laughed. "Same here. Gotta watch those seniors with their Kahluas and their troll dolls. A nasty combination when you're trying to maintain the peace."

Walter walked by and nodded to the men. "How's the food, boys?"

"Great," Billy said, "especially the shrimp." He put three in his mouth and chewed. A few seconds later, he emptied his glass of Chardonnay. "Thanks for the invitation."

"You're a friend of both Ted and Hank, you're welcome." Walter laughed. "Although, it's hard to imagine Hank anywhere near a casino. Too straitlaced."

"Hank, Ted, and I are softball buddies," Billy said, "Though it's mostly for the wings and beer afterward." He licked cocktail sauce from his fingers. "We also do a little hunting in the Pinelands, though Hank mostly comes for the peace and quiet after putting up with the construction noises." He bit into another shrimp. "Man, these are good."

"Funny," Ted said, his voice raised to muffle Billy's mastication. "I can't imagine Hank living in Kansas. Seems like a flat, desolate, landscape. A lot less interesting than Jersey."

Billy laughed. "I'm sure Hank found things to do there." He snorted. "I'd bet he also got into his share of trouble."

Walter smiled. "Who knows? Maybe enough trouble to make him leave and come to Long Harbor."

• • • • •

The hostess switched on her microphone. "Ladies and gentlemen, the tables are now ready for dinner. You'll find place cards on the tables just inside the dining room. Please enjoy your evening and celebrate the lovely couple and this fine day."

Ted nodded to the men and walked to the corridor to join Hank, Sue and the bridal party preparing to be announced. Walter spotted Nancy and the proud parents hurried to their ringside table. Billy found his card and searched for Table 8. In no time, he was chatting up a redhead who appeared to be without a plus one. "Must be his natural hunting instincts," Hank said to Ted as they watched the charmer pull out her chair and say something that made her smile.

"A good man to know," said Ted. "And a better ally."

$$\bullet \quad \bullet \quad \bullet \quad \bullet \quad \bullet$$

After introductions, the bridal party and the attendees sat and chatted. Ted pulled a paper from his coat pocket, took a sip of water, then walked to the mic. He tapped his glass. When everyone quieted, Ted cleared his throat and motioned to the couple. "Folks, today we celebrate Hank and Sue, partners in life and sometimes crime." A laugh. "And two of the nicest people you'd ever meet." Applause. "To use a football term, and as anyone who has met the pair knows, Hank certainly outkicked his coverage. Sue is kind, witty, smart, and beyond generous."

He turned to his best friend and shook his head. "Then, there's Hank: Junk food junkie, football fan, and the world's worst poker player." He leaned into Sue's hearing but aimed his words for all. "He has a *tell*, Sue. He raises one eyebrow when he has a good hand. When he's bluffing, he scratches his nose. Be gentle with him, Sue. He's really a good guy, just a lousy bluff. If he tells you something, you know he's lying if he scratches his schnoz."

He raised his glass. "Everyone, to the finest couple you'd ever have the good fortune to meet, I ask you to toast Hank and Sue Malone, two of Long Harbor's finest citizens. Here's hoping I never have to arrest them."

Laughter, a mumble of agreement, then downing of champagne. "Now for the prayer before our fine meal, I'd like to quote Hank in one of his inspired moments of religious fervor." Ted folded his hands and bowed his head. The guests followed. "Past the teeth and over the gums. Watch out stomach, here it comes."

$$\bullet \quad \bullet \quad \bullet \quad \bullet \quad \bullet$$

The party lasted late into the night. Remarkably, no one got drunk, though raised voices debated whether the Giants would beat the Eagles this year. Little interest in the Jets, though Sue put on eye grease after a trip to the ladies' room, and led a small contingent into a chant of "Jets, Jets, Jets."

Ted, Nick, Luciano, Maurice, and Hank posed with Sue and the bridesmaids sitting in the middle. Hank noticed that Luciano and Maurice kept their distance from each other, while maintaining the camaraderie of the event. They both looked at Nick with masked unease. How did this newcomer become so influential in the construction of the Town Centre? Clearly, Hank's star pupil. The two men put on a good face when posing with Hank and Sue, but the mistrust was clear.

Nick brought over Gina, his date for the wedding. Ted motioned Rhonda, his wife, to join in, and Billy Whitedeer came over with his tablemate, Linda, a friend of Walter and Nancy. Nieces and nephews were rounded up and posed in front of the adults.

More photos until Hank and Sue had no one else to share the occasion with except the busboys. What the heck, they joined in a Kodak moment with the couple.

Guests filtered out after final hugs and handshakes. Walter, Nancy, Hank, and Sue thanked each member of the wedding party, then only they remained, spending time together until the hostess hinted at closing. The four left, talked in the parking lot for another half hour, then Mr. and Mrs. Malone drove home to share their wedded bliss, and open the envelopes containing best wishes and wedding loot.

Hank shaved, dabbed on cologne, and laid on the bed in his cleanest boxers. Sue came out of the bathroom wearing Hank's Eagles jersey and nothing else. The game was on.

CHAPTER 28

Hank and Sue returned from a week in Cape May. Sue resumed her head nurse duties in Memorial Hospital, clearly missed by the staff and doctors.

Hank met with Maurice Lobo, who had filled in for the week. Maurice gave Hank a detailed status, including frank assessments of the interactions among workforces.

Town Centre was progressing with no disruptions caused by Hank's absence. The signage for the Amazon store was up and there was buzz that Jeff Bezos himself would appear for the grand opening. The Amazon Building Services management in Newark were watching the construction closely. This would be a feather in the cap for their construction venture in the Northeast.

The Smith crew continued their diligent work. Nick was officially named as lead, replacing Stan Cummings, who returned to the Camden ward, counting time until his retirement. Everyone knew that Nick was the de facto face of Smith, anyway. Stan signed timesheets but Nick did the heavy lifting, including trying to keep the interaction with the Amazon and Gallante workers professional, if not always cordial.

The Gallante team kept up with the plumbing installations and maintained what appeared to be a respectful coexistence with the Smith carpenters and Amazon electricians and masons. Mike Angeloni seemed to be assuming an influential, if unofficial, role, though his whispered conversations with other tradesmen, caused some unease for Luciano.

Hank thanked Maurice for his brutal honesty and for running the construction in his stead. He sent Maurice back to the Amazon storefront to oversee the final touches.

Opening his laptop, Hank swiveled his chair to regain the muscle memory in his gluteus, and opened his email app. Dozens of congratulatory notes were unopened, awaiting his response. He took time to answer each, then put on his hard hat and left to check the construction first-handed.

The Harry Winston, Amazon, Gucci, and Cheesecake Factory storefronts were glass and steel marvels of engineering. Plenty of light, open space undergoing landscaping, and tasteful signage, more of a "Welcome, friend" approach than a "Hey, look at me."

Pneumatic drills competed with the bang of hammers as the inside of each store was readied for a pre-Christmas opening. A twelve foot tall Santa's sleigh, connected to reindeer harnesses, stood on the future Main Street, awaiting electrical connection and piped-in music. A hand-painted logo of Mr. Claus grinned through his plastic weatherproofing, seeming to know that he would soon be the guest of honor at the Christmas parade.

As he walked down the yet-to-be-paved thoroughfare, Hank imagined crowds of happy consumers carrying overstuffed shopping bags, posing for selfies with their children, and enjoying the miniature city of commerce.

A police cruiser followed him. Hank turned to see Ted, who smiled at his friend as he stopped the Tesla Model S, donated by the manufacturer. He jumped out and hugged Hank. "Welcome back, Hank. How was Cape May?"

"A little cold and fairly empty in the offseason, but still a great getaway." He turned and looked around. "I'm not sure I was missed. This place seems to run itself."

"Only because Hank Malone is running his little league of nations with a firm but fair hand," Ted said. "And with our quiet oversight."

Hank wasn't sure what that meant.

"Frankly, Hank, I expected more rancor among the tradesmen. We do have our eyes on some of the Gallante folks since they're known for a short fuse, the Amazonians always have this glassy expression in their eyes, and the Mormons seem too pleasant to be real. There must be a current of emotion underneath."

"I'm guessing there is, Ted," Hank said. "Let's hope the Christmas season has a calming effect and keeps any unpleasantness under wraps."

• • • • •

The late November skies were filled with clouds overstuffed with moisture. "Feels like snow," was muttered by shivering guests as they lined Main Street waiting for the Christmas parade to begin. Billy Whitedeer examined his image in the dressing room mirror. "Ho, Ho, Ho, everyone. Merry Christmas," he practiced. Ted and Hank both laughed. "Perfect, Billy," said Ted. "They'll never know it's you."

"I hope the reindeer think it's Santa. I can't believe you got actual antlered deer."

"Did you know, Billy," Hank said, "that only female adult reindeer have antlers?" He laughed. "You'll be leading a group of cows, that's what they're called, down the parade route."

"I hope they're steadier than I am. I've never driven a sleigh before."

Nick, Maurice, and Luciano walked in, closing the door quickly before the newly arriving flakes could rush in.

"I didn't know it snowed this early in Jersey," Nick said. "Feels more like Utah out there."

'Or even Washington state," added Maurice.

Luciano removed a flask from under his coat. "Jersey folk are ready for anything Mother Nature can throw at them." He found paper cups and poured a libation for each man. Nick hesitated, then lifted his drink also as Luciano offered a toast. "To the success of Town Centre, an engineering marvel built by people as diverse as they come."

"Hear, hear," they all responded. The whiskey went down each throat, Nick taking only a sip, followed by a sequence of "Ah's." Billy declined a refill. "Can't have Santa staggering to his sleigh. Rudolph, or Rudolphina, I guess, would never forgive me."

Sue walked in, sniffed and grabbed a paper cup. "I smell whiskey. "If I'm gonna be Mrs. Claus, I'll need something to keep me warm." Luciano poured, stopping at half full. "Uh, Uh, Sancti," she said. "I need enough to warm my toes, too."

He continued to dispense, emptying the flask and allowing the last few drops to drip into her cup to show he wasn't holding back. "Done, Mrs. Claus."

Sue emptied the cup in seconds. "Ah, good stuff. I'll soon be ready for battle."

Nick poured the remainder of his drink into her glass. "Good man, Olsen." She chugged it down. "Now I'm ready."

Hank checked his watch. "Showtime, gentlemen, and lady. Let's do Town Centre proud."

●   ●   ●   ●   ●

"And here they come, folks: Santa, Mrs. Claus, and their beautiful elves. The first annual Town Centre Christmas Parade is about to begin," said Tornado O'Reilly, WLH-TV weatherman and reporter. He gestured the cameraman to zoom in on the entourage. "Whoa, what's this? Mrs. Claus is laying a big kiss on Hank Malone, construction supervisor of Town Centre." He laughed. "I hope Santa isn't the jealous type."

Hank was resisting Mrs. Claus's overture. Fortunately, his face was obstructed by the two-handed smooch being applied to him. "Back to the parade, Tornado," a voice whispered, no doubt the WLH-TV producer on site.

"And there goes Santa up on his sleigh, assisted by six elves. Mrs. Claus is following, rejecting offers of aid from Santa's Helpers." Tornado snorted. "I think it's going to be even colder at the North Pole tonight."

Workers connected the harnesses from the reindeer to the sleigh after calming the animals who seemed intent on stampeding. "Ho, Ho, Ho," Santa called to the crowd. "Merry Christmas to everyone."

A man in blue overalls patted the first reindeer, and summoned the rest to follow him. The slack in the harnesses tightened and the animals started to pull the sleigh. "Now, folks," Tornado continued, "I'll let you in on a little secret. I guess you're wondering how the sleigh is moving with just a thin layer of snow on the ground. Well, there are wheels under the conveyance." He leaned into the camera so close, the cameraman needed to back up slightly. "Don't tell anyone, especially the kiddos."

Billy Whitedeer, AKA Santa, greeted the crowd. "Ho, Ho, Ho, the parade is on its way. Welcome, everyone, to Town Centre."

Mrs. Claus stood, fell back into her seat, and grabbed Santa's coat for support. "Merry Christmas, everyone," she shouted, causing the crowd closest to the speakers to cover their ears.

Hank ran beside the sleigh, his hat blowing off, and face exposed. He said something to Mrs. Claus. "Oops," she said, covering her mouth. "Mrs. Claus needs to use her inside voice today."

•   •   •   •   •

Charlie Benner lowered the sound on his flat screen, drank the remaining bourbon in his glass, and sighed. "Man, Hank would have been more concealed if he actually played Santa. At least the beard would have covered his face. He's one facial profile away from getting yanked out of Long Harbor." He glanced at his car keys resting on the end table. "If his sudden disappearance wouldn't cause concern and publicity, I'd be driving down there now."

He refilled his glass, swirled and sipped. "C'mon, Santa, start throwing candy canes. Anything to get Hank off the screen."

•   •   •   •   •

The Warrior Room in Lenape Casino was filling with guests dressed in their finery for the First Annual Town Centre Employee Christmas Party. Yesterday's Christmas parade was praised on social media, newsprint, and radio from as far away as Cambria, 40 miles north. The partygoers were ready to toast the success with free top-shelf liquor, appetizers, a sit-down dinner, and dancing.

Jeff Bezos tweeted his congratulations and wished the management and crew a well-deserved celebration for making Town Centre the crown jewel of South Jersey upscale shopping.

Bishop Shumway of the Philadelphia Temple sent his blessings and a gold-leafed book of Mormon. Mario Gallante, emeritus head of the South Jersey mob, sent his greetings and contributed a door prize, an oil painting of Fat Elvis sweating over an adoring crowd.

Billy Whitedeer stood at the entrance to the ballroom, wearing his best suit with the Lenape Casino logo in royal blue displayed on his pocket square. Italians, Mormons, Amazonians, and respective wives and girlfriends, smiled to the six foot four inch purebred Lenape Indian.

Hank and Sue stood near the open bar and watched the line of well-dressed union tradesmen and managers entering the ballroom with their dates. Ted Hanson appeared with his wife Rhonda, found Hank and walked over. Men steered their dates toward the appetizer table when they recognized Rhonda, resplendent in a tight black dress, a far cry from her G-string worn at Birds of a Feather, her prior employer. "Don't let them intimidate you, Rhonda," Ted said as he, Billy, Hank, and Sue watched the walk of the shamed.

"That's OK, Ted," she said. "If they give me any grief, I'll write their sins in the dust."

The lights dimmed. "And now ladies and gentlemen, please take your seats as we introduce to you our emcee for the evening, Murray the Magnificent."

The crowd applauded as they found their tables. A tuxedoed man bounded on to the stage and raised his arm. A dove appeared in his palm, left his hand and flew high over the guests. He, she, or it returned to Murray's outstretched baton, alighted, and cooed. "Everyone, say hello to Lady Dove," After polite applause, he motioned to the bird and a large cloud of smoke enveloped it. When the smoke cleared, Lady Dove was gone, replaced by a blond, black woman in a white satin sparkling gown. The men stood and cheered. The ladies signaled the men to resume their seats.

Billy walked toward the dais. "And now, folks," Murray continued, "our kind host, and general manager of Lenape casino, Mr. Billy Whitedeer," The women stood and cheered.

Billy raised both arms and gestured to the ornate surroundings. "Thank you, everyone, and welcome to Lenape Casino — now the second-most famous landmark in Long Harbor."

The crowd applauded.

"Tonight, we celebrate two years of hard work, cooperation and skilled labor, vital to the construction of Town Centre."

He held out his hand and pointed to Hank. "Brought together by this humble man who made sure everyone focused on the common goal. Ladies and gentlemen, let's hear it for Hank Malone, construction foreman for Town Centre."

Hank walked to the dais, head bowed, but determined to speak. "Hello, everyone. Thanks for all of the great work over this year. We completed a project only dreamed of years ago." He waited for the polite applause to finish. "And, we did it on time and under budget with great dedication from our unions, and the support of the Long Harbor government and business community." Louder applause, with the table of city leaders and the chamber of commerce standing and waving to the guests.

"And, as a special surprise, our government and business leaders have promised a two week Christmas bonus to all of our memberships." The leaders seemed puzzled, but hearing the cheers and whistles, waved again. Hank smiled at the spontaneous trickledown economics he had just imposed. "So, everyone, raise your glasses to the city fathers, business leaders, Amazon, Smith Engineering, Gallante Plumbing, all our tradesman, and to the successful future of Town Centre."

Everyone got to their feet. Hank could have been carried off and made king at that point, but then remembered he was a wanted man on the run. "So, let's hit the buffet tables, the open bar, and the dance floor. Tonight, we celebrate."

●　　●　　●　　●　　●

Charlie Benner returned from Sunday Mass, placed his bacon McGriddle, hash browns, donut sticks, and coffee on his kitchen table, removed his snow-covered gloves and parka, and opened his Sunday paper. The front page told of world leaders threatening the peace, the environment, or encouraging general mayhem. Charlie sighed and leafed through the massive Long Harbor Press until he found the Local News section.

Above the fold was a full-color photo of his main client, Hank Malone, the former Louie Kimball. "Shit," he said, loud enough to cause his cat to run for cover. "C'mon Hank, can't you blend into the background like a good witness?"

He read the accompanying story. "Well, Hank, you're a big man on campus now," he whispered. His cell rang. Reading the incoming number, he sighed and answered. "Bureau chief Baker. How are you on this lovely winter Sunday morning? A little crisp for my liking, but there you go."

A harrumph on the line. "Charlie, I got a call from D.C, I was told to go online and check out The Long Harbor Press. Our guest is becoming quite the local celebrity. D.C. is getting nervous. Bad karma having one of our star witnesses become the toast of the town. What's next, the Nobel Prize?"

Charlie picked up a donut stick, dunked it in his coffee and took a bite, hoping for inspiration.

"Benner, are you there?"

He swallowed, then coughed from the combination of greasy pastry and strong coffee. "Sid, I know it doesn't look good. I'll have a talk with him. He won't be willing to leave town, I know that."

"Tell him that if he still wants protection, he'll have to either leave or wise up." A snort on the line. "Otherwise, we remove his protection and tell him he has to fend for himself."

CHAPTER 29

Hank sipped his caramel macchiato and leafed through the paper. Starbucks was filled with excited customers. He eavesdropped to pass the time. College kids meeting up with old friends, girlfriends showing each other their Christmas purchases. *Oh, yes, and a fugitive from the Mormon mob meeting his FBI handler.*

Charlie Benner held a peppermint latte in one hand and a slice of lemon cake in the other. He peered over the sitting area, in search of an empty chair. Hank sighed. *This is Déjà vu all over again.* Charlie pointed to the seat across from Hank. "Is this taken, young man?"

"Be my guest."

The agent, who was only a few years older than Hank, placed his lunch on the table. Hank started to talk, but Charlie raised his hand and walked over to a counter, grabbed a dozen napkins, as many stirrers, and a fistful of sugar packets.

He returned, dumped his loot on the table, and sat. "I appreciate this. Looks like it's the busy season."

Hank checked his immediate vicinity and leaned forward. "The last time someone joined me in Starbucks, it was our friend, Nelson. I'm guessing these are similar circumstances."

Charlie looked around, scoping out any neighbors who might be listening. "I'm afraid so. You keep showing up on TV and the papers. For late December, it's getting awful warm, if you know what I mean."

"I'm not leaving, Charlie. I've put down roots here. I have a wife, a good job, and, I'm in the lottery for playoff tickets."

"Understood, Hank. But I have to tell you, if you don't leave town and let us find you safer surroundings, we're going to consider dropping you from the program." He sipped his drink. "And you'll be on your own."

"Are our friends still in prison?"

"All except Carlos Garcia. He got out on parole. Wears an ankle bracelet and has to stick to Utah for the next couple years."

"Am I even on the radar?"

"Big time, Hank. They don't forget their enemies. I wouldn't be surprised if your likeness was plastered on the walls of each meetinghouse in the country. Might even be one in Camden."

"But I got the bad guys arrested. Doesn't that count for anything?"

"Religion is big on external forgiveness, Hank. But I always thought that the internal need for retribution is common to most belief systems. Maybe I'm a pessimist, but you're not in the clear by any stretch." He took another sip, wiped whipped cream from his lips, and picked up the paper. He found Hank's picture and the article on Town Centre. "That's why Hank Malone, and Louie Kimball, have to leave and leave soon."

Hank collected his paper and stood. "I'm staying, Charlie. So is Louie."

•　　•　　•　　•　　•

"How was the get together with your friend?" Sue asked, placing a bookmark into her latest mystery novel. She lifted her Heineken and took a long chug.

Hank sat on the couch, twisted off the cap of his Flying Fish, and pushed the cat away before it could lay claim to his lap. "Much like I expected, I'm afraid." He sat forward. "Sue ..."

His wife raised a hand, dug her back scratcher into the chair cushions and pulled out her car keys. She held them up like a prized bass. "It just occurred to me where they might be. Things are always falling out of these pants."

"My wife, the detective." He took a sip of his pilsner. "Sue, I just met with the FBI."

"The FBI? What for, Hank?" She swung herself out of the cozy chair and walked over to him. She pushed the cat off the couch and sat. "Are you in any trouble? Is something going on at Town Centre?"

"Remember when I asked you in Giorgio's if you wanted to leave town with me?"

Sue rubbed her chin. "That was over a year ago. I thought we discussed that." She turned to face him completely. "What's going on, Hank?"

"Let me get us a few more beers. This might take a while."

●   ●   ●   ●   ●

Sue thought over what Hank told her. She put the empty bottle on a coaster, took a breath, and then punched him in the arm, hard enough to cause the Flying Fish to drop into his lap. It landed vertically, Hank closing his thighs to catch the bottle. "I deserve that, Sue. I've made a mess of things."

"What do we do now? Just pack up and leave?"

Hank shook his head. "No, I told Charlie, he's my FBI handler, that I'm not running anymore. I'm in this for good. I'm not disappearing."

"Louie Kimball, huh," Sue said, trying out the sound of it. "I prefer Hank Malone."

"So do I, and I love this life we have. I'm not giving it up."

"And Nick doesn't know who you are?" She laughed, her nerves apparent. "Boy, you must have crapped your pants when you saw him at your front door, then at the construction site a few days later."

"I don't think he recognized me as Louie. I had plastic surgery, like I said. They did a good job, straightened out my chin."

Sue picked up the beer from Hank's lap and took a swig. "Funny, when I first checked over the printed wedding announcement with my parents, my dad remarked that from the side you resembled Wally, a pet ferret I had as a kid." She put her hand on his shoulder. Hank flinched, anticipating another left hook. "My dad wasn't criticizing, just making an observation."

"Great," Hank said. "I wonder who else noticed."

•   •   •   •   •

Monday morning. Hank entered his new office in the management building. He swiveled in his rolling chair, stirred his coffee, and admired his surroundings. *A far cry from the construction trailer. I could get used to this.* He frowned. *If I wasn't a wanted man.* He checked the appointment page of his email: a 10 o'clock meeting with the project managers, and a hastily arranged 11:30 meeting with his construction leaders.

Nick knocked on the door and stood until Hank motioned him in." "Wow, Hank. This is nice. You deserve this." He walked to the window, and watched shoppers already arriving in the new parking lot. "It's gratifying when a good guy gets his reward. Makes the rest of us know that we get what's coming to us, if we just persist."

Hank sighed. "Nick, you're right. We get what we deserve."

He swung his chair and pointed to the construction trailer, now in a corner dwarfed by the completed storefronts. "Nick, as I've been promoted into management, we need someone to make sure the construction and maintenance work continues to get done. I've recommended you for foreman."

Nick sat forward. "Hank, this is a real honor. Are you sure Luciano and Maurice are OK with this?"

"They'll have to be, Nick. Only room for one alpha dog. I'll let them know after I finish with the 10 o'clock management meeting."

Nick was quiet, taking it in. "I wouldn't have appointed you, Nick, if I didn't think you could handle it," Hank said, patting him on the shoulder. He opened a spreadsheet on his laptop. "Now, let's go over the accounts and personnel information." He typed in the password. "Oh, by the way, the password is "coolhandluke.""

•   •   •   •   •

The management team sat in silence when Hank suggested Nick as his replacement. Mayor Evers Wilson, director of the civil/business enterprise, sat up and tapped his pen on the notepad.

"I don't know, Hank. Young Olsen is certainly a credit to the project and his leadership of the Smith team has allowed for a smooth work environment, but do you think he's ready to manage this diverse group of tradesmen?"

"I'm certain he can handle it," Hank said. "Frankly, it's the best choice. We don't want to name someone from Gallante. They always seem to be in the middle of any upheaval, and there's too much negative history of them in this town for it not to smell rotten. And Amazon, an interesting approach maybe, but a little too robotic for South Jersey."

He walked to the window and watched as shoppers walked from the parking lots to the stores. "Now, the Smith people, Mormons as you know, present an interesting contrast. Squeaky clean, hardworking, and teetotalers. A group we can present to future investors as representing our values."

Evers stood and joined Hank, watching the flow of happy customers. "I remember a scandal with them years ago. A Nevada desert project, which got busted by the FBI." He put his hand on Hank's shoulder. Hank flinched but composed himself. "How do we know this won't become more of the same when Nick's leading the troops?"

"Nick's not that kind of guy, Mayor Evers. He would stop any such activity before it got out of hand."

"OK, Hank. Just keep an eye on things from a distance. We don't need another crime spree or scandal in this town. Make sure your example of right and wrong helps young Olsen keep to the steady path. Show the young man how a good man of faith like yourself can resist the temptations of money and power. Make Hank Malone his shining example of uncorrupted leadership."

Hank sighed. "Will do, Mayor Evers. Don't worry about what happened in Nevada years ago. It's South Jersey now. It's a different time and place."

•　　•　　•　　•　　•

Hank called Luciano, Maurice, and Nick into his office. The men swiveled in the new cushioned chairs, and enjoyed the panoramic view of the center, with Long Harbor, and then the ocean, in the distance. A caterer walked in and placed a tray of sandwiches, chips, drinks, and deserts on the table.

"Dig in, guys. Straight from Primo's."

The men piled food on their plates. "And there's plenty more for your men. It's being delivered now."

Talk centered on the Predators, currently in first place, and favored to compete for the Super Bowl. "Some men are already talking of spending their Christmas bonus on playoff tickets," Luciano said. "That is, if their wives don't object."

"There should be enough left to get something nice for the wife," Maurice said. "Say something from, I don't know, the Amazon store?" The men laughed.

"Or Harry Winston," Hank said. "Something to warm up even cold winter nights."

Silence as the men dove into their lunch. The ritual of greedily consuming a free business meal outweighed any need for human interaction. Hank watched Luciano and Maurice, then glanced over to Nick who seemed anxious as he played with his Italian hoagie.

Hank stood and walked to the whiteboard. He wrote out a list of remaining work and maintenance functions for each of the major trade groups, using purple for Gallante, green for Smith Enterprises, and orange for Amazon. He then created a separate column for Oversight and chose black.

"Men, Town Centre has come a long way in these two years. When I started, the foreman, Larry Marino, showed me around and painted a glowing picture of what the completed product would look like and what it would do for Long Harbor."

He picked up a Ring Ding, took a few seconds to delight in the chocolate marvel, and, in three bites, finished it off. Wiping his hands in a napkin, he picked up the black marker again. "With the cooperation of our trade groups, we were able to accomplish Larry's vision. Now, except for some final cleanup, we're in maintenance mode."

He waved his arms, indicating his new workplace. "I've been kicked upstairs, placed on the management track, and asked to name a successor as foreman."

Each man put down their lunch and sat back. "I've decided on Nick Olsen. He'll start as foreman this week, and we'll determine the Smith successor."

Luciano tapped the desk. "I'm not sure how Gallante management and the men will react to this, Hank. I'm already getting internal pressure to make Gallante more prominent. This won't go down well." He turned to Nick. "No offense, Nick. It's just that we expected someone more local to take Hank's place." He laughed. "And you're not even a *goombah*. In South Jersey, that's a rarity. We accepted Hank since he's a good Catholic boy, but you're going to be a tougher sell."

Maurice stopped playing with a Tastykake, stood, and cleared his throat. Luciano stopped talking. "We at Amazon Building Services have great plans for South Jersey. Town Centre has been a good inroad for us and we have learned many lessons about getting along with others. Like Luciano says, this may not sit well with company management and the rank and file, but I'll smooth things over as well as I can." He unwrapped the Butterscotch Krimpet and licked the icing. "Congratulations, Nick," he said, the words muffled somewhat.

Luciano murmured, "Congratulations," and opened a bag of chips.

"Well, there you have it, guys. I'll give you time to tell your teams," Hank said. "Let's keep Town Centre moving forward together."

A well-dressed woman knocked at the door, accompanied by a heavily bearded and unkempt man holding a camera. "Hi, I'm Lisa Channing from The Long Harbor Press. This is my associate, Ricky Barnes. We're doing a story on the completion of Town Centre and the public relations department sent us here."

Hank introduced his team and explained the celebration. "Great," said Lisa. "Let's get a group photo. All of South Jersey will see the men who built this new amazing landmark."

Ricky had already grabbed a roast beef sandwich and a Dr. Pepper. Lisa shook her head. "Excuse my cameraman. He doesn't like to miss a free meal."

The men laughed and formed around Lisa. Ricky licked the mayo from his fingers, wiped his hands on his shirt, and picked up his camera. "Say Long Harbor," he said, a piece of beef dangling between his teeth.

Hanks sighed. *A fugitive mugging for the camera. Charlie will probably have a heart attack.*

●   ●   ●   ●   ●

The Gallante crew mumbled their disbelief to Luciano's news. "That should have been you, Luciano," Mike Angeloni said. "We handle all of the plumbing in this place. They can't take a crap without us. What do the Smith people do besides put up walls and cabinets? Besides, the guy is younger than I am."

Luciano sat on the edge of his desk. "I don't know why Hank picked such a young guy to replace him, but that's how the shit stuck on the wall. Gallante still has influence here, and we don't want to upset things ... for now. Let the Amazons stew over this. We'll get our chance later on, especially if Amazon oversteps or young Nick falters."

Mike and other men started whispering among themselves. "And we're *not* going to help him falter, men. No dirty tricks, no sudden water shutoffs. We play this by the book. If we need to put pressure on later, we do it from a higher level. We're not goons here ... not yet."

●   ●   ●   ●   ●

Maurice met with his men and announced the change. Most of the workers were surprised, some indignant.

"Let's give Olsen a chance to get a footing. There's no reason to rock the boat here. Corporate can impose influence on the town fathers, if need be. For now, it would be better if we just played this out."

"What about the Gallante men? What do they think?" a welder called out from the back of the room.

"We'll find out in the next few days," Maurice said. "Head cracking is more in their wheelhouse. Maybe this will help us to elbow out the plumbers. We do our job, and await events. Who knows, this could be an opportunity being dropped into our laps. We watch our competition destroy themselves." He pointed to the framed portrait on the wall. "Just like our leader does."

CHAPTER 30

Carlos Garcia opened the mailbox outside his late mother's West Jordan, Utah, rancher. The manila envelope jammed on the metal edges as he struggled to remove it. He grunted and placed his just delivered pizza on the curb, needing to devote two hands to the task.

He unfolded the brown wrapper and read the return address. "Ah, Aunt Mildred from Jersey," he mumbled. He tried to judge the weight. "Not too heavy. I wonder what she sent me now."

He placed the mail on top of his pizza, obscuring the smiling man in the orange tunic. He walked to his front door, and juggling his keys, dropped most of the mail on the ground. The envelope remained, seemingly stuck to the top of the pizza box.

Going inside, he sighed at the blast of air-conditioning, a welcome relief from the ninety- five degree sweat fest outside. He picked up the envelope and, grabbing a paper towel, brushed the grease from the back. Tearing the top, he shook until the contents fell out on the table. A note on Aunt Mildred's lavender notepaper, and a newspaper section.

Dearest Carlos:

I hope all is well. Enclosed is a news article and photo featuring my sister's boy Nicky. He's a hotshot in Long Harbor and was just promoted to construction foreman at a high-end shopping center called Town Centre. It just opened. In the picture, he is shown with his coworkers and his boss, a nice man named Hank Malone.

I wish you could visit us sometime. I know you can't leave Utah for a while, but maybe someday soon you can see us in New Jersey.

Your loving Aunt Mildred.

Carlos picked up a piece of pizza, blew on it and took a bite. He unfolded the Local News section and examined the photo. Nick, his nephew, beamed as he stood with his coworkers. He studied Nick for a few seconds. "Wow, he's grown up," he whispered. He read the caption, looking at each man as he matched the names listed left to right.

He viewed Hank Malone. Nice looking guy, he thought. Putting on his reading glasses, he focused on Hank only. "Huh! Where have I seen him before?" Moving his head back and forth to check the man at all angles, he put his pizza slice down and leaned forward, his nose inches from the newsprint. "Shit! Can that be who I think it is?"

He took out his cell and googled Louie Kimball. News articles from the trial came up. He examined pictures of Louie, his weasel-like visage prominent. He compared the photos to the one in the Long Harbor Press. "Hmm. Could be if they did some work on him?"

He found the newspaper's website and searched for Town Centre. Plenty of articles. The shopping venue was apparently a big deal. He paged through each seeking pictures of Hank Malone. He examined each one, checking the different angles of his face.

"Well, well, looks like I may have hit the jackpot. If that's Louie, he'll have a price on his head, and I can get my revenge."

He dialed his lawyer. "Hey, Pete, I know I'm stuck here in Utah, but I need to travel to New Jersey soon on an important family matter. Is there any chance you can check with the judge to loosen up my travel restrictions?"

• • • • •

Pete called back an hour later. "You have to give the reason in writing, Carlos. Be assured that they'll check on it to make sure you're not scamming the system."

Carlos thought this over. "And if I wait things out?"

"You're good to travel in a year. You'll still be on parole but no travel restrictions."

"OK, Pete. Thanks. I'll work something out with my family."

Carlos hung up and reexamined the pictures of Hank. "That's him, dammit. He better be around a year from now."

He found a blank piece of paper and a ballpoint that still had ink.

Dear Aunt Mildred:

It's nice to know that Nicky is doing so well in South Jersey. His Uncle Carlos is proud. It's a shame I can't come to visit, but am restricted to Utah by my parole. In a year, I can travel out of state. I plan to visit New Jersey and greet Nicky and the rest of my East Coast family.

Your loving nephew,
Carlos.

Carlos sealed the envelope, stamped it, and started to walk to his mailbox. He stopped in the hallway, noticing that he had tomato sauce on his BYU polo, right above the belly button. He licked the stain, hoping to avoid changing his favorite shirt. No luck. He wiggled out of the XXXL and found the *I Love New Jersey* tee that Aunt Mildred had sent a year ago when he got out of prison.

He laughed and checked himself in the mirror. "So, one year to work out a plan. One year till I get my hands on Louie Kimball," he whispered. "Now, Hank Malone, model citizen of Long Harbor, New Jersey."

CHAPTER 31

Nick poured more wine for Gina, then refilled his water glass. "I can't believe we've only been dating for a few months," Gina said. "I feel so comfortable with you."

"I know, Gina. I feel the same way." Nick looked around La Scala. "And this is our favorite place." Dean Martin's voice came over the sound system singing *That's Amore*.

"Just like Hank and Sue," Gina said. "And now they're married."

Nick put his glass down. "Listen, Gina. I'm not one to hide my feelings. I've enjoyed our time together." He took a breath. "And now I think I might be in love with you."

Whatsa Matta You replaced *That's Amore*.

"Do you feel the same way?"

"Are you kidding, Nick? I want to jump over the table and kiss you right here and now."

Nick reddened as the elderly couple at the next table turned and reacted to the direct answer. He reached for the remaining half-bottle of wine and offered it to the pair. "Please have this on us, folks. My girlfriend here may have had too much."

Gina opened her purse, took out a hundred-dollar bill, laid it on the table and stood. "I hope you both enjoy the wine. My boyfriend and I have to leave for private conversation."

The man gave Nick the thumbs-up. Nick stood, leaning on the table to quell his enthusiasm. "Enjoy your wine, folks."

Gina called from across the room, near the doorway. "Are you going to join me, Nick Olsen?"

Nick shrugged to the waiter as he collected the money.

"What are you waiting for, sir?" the waiter said. "Sounds like you have a much better offer."

$\bullet \quad \bullet \quad \bullet \quad \bullet \quad \bullet$

Gina's apartment. Nick turned on his back and caught his breath as Gina nuzzled in..

"I guess they never taught you that in divinity school, Nick. We East Coast girls are pretty direct."

He sighed. "I guess I have a lot to learn. I'm not in Utah anymore."

"I'll bring you along slowly, young Olsen. Just leave it to me."

$\bullet \quad \bullet \quad \bullet \quad \bullet \quad \bullet$

Monday morning. Hank, Luciano, and Maurice waited for Nick in Hank's office. "It's not like him to be late," Hank said, "especially for the monthly status meeting with the construction crews."

The door opened with a whoosh and Nick hurried in. "Sorry, I'm late. I overslept." The three men looked at each other, confused.

"Hey, that coffee smells good." Nick laughed. "I'm not supposed to drink it, but, boy, I could stand some."

Nick filled a cup and sat. He noticed the confusion of his associates. "What?"

Luciano leaned forward, finally understanding. "You got laid!" He sat back. "Good for you."

Hank studied Nick. "You were going slow with Gina. I guess things heated up."

"Geez, guys. Can't a guy come in happy on a Monday?"

The three men were silent.

"OK, I guess not. Listen, I'm not comfortable discussing my love life. Let's just say Gina and I had a great weekend."

Hank's cell rang. "Hi, Sue." He laughed. "We just heard."

Nick sighed.

"Listen, Sue. We had to drag it out of him. He was a perfect gentleman. Tell Gina that." He chuckled. "OK, see you later."

After Hank hung up, Nick opened his laptop. "Hank, is it OK if we start now? This is embarrassing."

"Agreed," said Maurice. "If young Nick happened to get lucky once over the weekend, it's not for us to dwell on it, or embarrass him."

"Four times," Nick mumbled.

"Damn," the three men said in unison. "How are you still walking," Luciano said.

"And how is Gina still walking," Hank said. Nick covered his eyes.

"You're right, Nick. It's none of our business. Gentlemen, let's start the meeting."

"Four times," mumbled Luciano. "Nick, you sure you're not Italian?"

•　　•　　•　　•　　•

Nick was a changed man. He took firm control of his own meetings, demanded strict accountability from all of the tradesmen, and presented his reports to Hank earlier than expected. He *did* tend to leave work at a reasonable hour, forsaking his previous long days.

Gina moved into his bayside apartment that weekend and reorganized his bachelor system of strewn clothes and unwashed dishes into a domestic habitat worthy of visitors and the occasional door-to-door solicitor. Nick now understood the intrusion he made while preaching the word of God. You can't meet a missionary in boxers.

The pair joined Hank and Sue on the occasional Saturday night out. The dinners were cordial and fun, but the steamy phase of the relationship kept the lovers away from their friends most weekends. Hank and Sue were somewhat jealous, their status changing to "old married couple" when compared to Long Harbor's newest power pair.

One day, Gina came into work sporting a diamond ring. Sue and the team of nurses closed in, marveling at the setting as Gina turned her wrist to expose the sparkle under the harsh hospital lights.

"He took me to La Scala last night. He got on one knee and asked during *Shaddup You Face*. Everyone applauded. It was my dream come true."

Sue edged away from the circle of nurses, doctors, and patients, and called Hank.

"I know, Sue. Nick told me this morning," Hank said. "He's pretty excited and high-fiving any worker who passes by. It's hard to believe this is the same Nick who led a life of quiet reflection and dedicated purpose just six months or so ago."

'Remind me, Hank. Who set them up?"

"It was you, Sue. Matchmaker extraordinaire."

$$\bullet \qquad \bullet \qquad \bullet \qquad \bullet \qquad \bullet$$

The couple invited Hank and Sue over for dinner Tuesday evening. Gina cooked chicken cacciatore and fettuccine. Nick whipped up a Caesar salad. Chianti sealed the deal with Nick matching his guests drink for drink.

"Wow. This is definitely Nick Olsen 2.0," Hank said. "Self-assured and outgoing."

"And no slouch on the romantic end," Gina said.

Nick turned red. "Just manifesting my inner self," he responded.

The plates were cleared, and the four attacked a box of cannolis. Hank loosened his belt a notch when Nick and Gina walked to the kitchen.

"I saw that, Hank Malone," Sue said. "We need to hit the treadmills again."

Nick and Gina returned to the dining room, hand-in-hand. "So, we've been discussing our wedding plans," Gina said. "And we'd like Sue to be Maid of Honor."

"Wonderful," said Sue. "I'd be honored."

"And we'd like Hank to be Best Man," Nick said.

'Nick and Gina, it would be my distinct pleasure."

"We're thinking next June," said Gina. 'This gives us time to plan, create a guest list, select a venue, and book a honeymoon." She rubbed

Nick's shoulder. "This is all such a whirlwind. I told my parents, and they're contacting all of the relatives. Everyone's thrilled."

"And I've told my Aunt Mildred," Nick said. "She's thrilled and reaching out to family and friends. She's even in touch with my uncle from Salt Lake City. I haven't seen him in years." He took Gina's hand. "I hope he can make it. I owe him a real debt for helping me out when I was there for seminary school."

Hank lifted his glass. "Here's to meeting your fine families. I'm sure they'll look forward to sharing the joyous day and meeting your Long Harbor friends."

• • • • •

Carlos opened the envelope. Aunt Mildred with the next update from Jersey: glossy pictures of Nick and his intended attached to Mildred's lilac writing paper. He examined the photo. Pretty couple, he thought, as he picked up his Mountain Dew.

Dearest Carlos:

My Nicky is getting married! What a nice surprise. The girl is wonderful. An Italian and full of spirit. Not too many LDS women here in South Jersey, but that's OK, as long as he's happy.

Their wedding is set for next June, thirteen months from now. His Best Man will be Hank Malone, his boss and good friend from Long Harbor. His wife, Sue, will be Maid of Honor.

The weather should be nice and, hopefully, you can join us. And please bring a date. It should be a fun time enjoyed by all.

Stay well, nephew. Next June will be here before we know it. Nicky and his bride will be so thrilled to see you. I'm sure he'll introduce you to all of his friends in Town Centre.

Your loving Aunt Mildred.

Carlos laughed and took a sip of his drink. One year is not too long, according to Aunt Mildred, he thought. That works out just right for me, he thought, I don't think I'll let the church leadership know about this...for now. I can solve their missing Louie problem, for a reasonable fee of course. Or I can have Kimball make me a counteroffer. Looks like I hold all the cards.

Now, how to exterminate the rat without disrupting Nicky's wedding. Make him suddenly leave town before the ceremony, and then follow him to his demise? If I can't pull that off, then confront him quietly at the wedding.

I wonder who I can take with me. Someone who knows Louie would be a real surprise for him. Wait a minute, I know the perfect 'plus 1.' I hope she's still around.

CHAPTER 32

Nick stood outside Steve Yount's office in the Camden Ward, waiting for his monthly meeting with his leader and advisor. Steve was on the phone with Salt Lake City, and had Nick wait outside.

He looked over the cluttered bulletin board: announcements of upcoming meetings, items listed for sale, and a cartoon of a couple in Salt Lake City marveling at the buildings as they fanned themselves in the late summer heat.

At the top, a photo with the caption HAVE YOU SEEN ME? The man in the picture had a serious gaze, befitting a commitment to purpose. Identified as Elder Louie Kimball, the poster described the need to bring him to justice within the LDS community.

Nick moved closer to photo. Hey, wait a minute, he thought.

He took down the picture and sat on a nearby bench. That looks like Hank, he thought. It could be him if his appearance was smoothed out. Nick read the remainder of the description. Left Salt Lake City almost five years ago, could be anywhere. Urgent to find him.

Louie Kimball. Wait a minute, he thought. Louie 'The Ferret' Kimball? The man who testified against the LDS? And now they want him brought in?

He placed the flyer back into position, returned to the bench and thought this over. Stan Cummings walked by. "Nick Olsen. Good to see you here. How are things at Town Centre?"

Nick forced a smile. "Good, Leader Cummings." He looked around. "I'm waiting for Ward Leader Yount, he's on the phone." Nick stood. "Do you have a few minutes to talk?"

"Of course, young Nick. Follow me to my office."

The men walked into the small room, no more than ten feet wide. "My humble abode," Stan said. "Have a seat. What's up?"

"I was looking at the photo of Louie Kimball on the bulletin board outside of Steve's office."

"And..."

"Well, Leader Cummings, it looks like Hank Malone, if you smoothed out the facial features."

Stan left his chair and closed the office door. He walked to the window and watched the traffic navigating through the city. He turned to Nick. "And what if it is, Nick? What do you propose?"

Nick sat up. "Do you mean you think so, too?"

"I figured it out a few months after I started working with Hank." He shook his head. "I thought of turning him in, but he's such a genuine guy, I couldn't do it. Besides, what he did took courage. It's not easy to turn against your religious leaders. It's like you're renouncing your faith."

Nick walked over to the window. "The LDS has been my whole life, Leader Cummings. And now I have to choose between my friend and my religion."

"No, Nick. You have to choose between right and wrong. Between the powerful and your friends. The brotherhood is more than the people who run it. It's folks like yourself and other clear minded men and women who need to stand up for what's right."

A knock on the door. "Is Elder Olsen in there, Stan? He has a meeting with me."

"That's Yount, Nick. He's waiting. It's up to you to decide what to do. I can't advise you on this. You need to look into your soul." He patted Nick on the shoulder. "Now, on your way."

Nick walked to the door. Hank's my friend, he thought. I'll have to hold on to this information while I think this over. Am I serving God or my leaders in Salt Lake?

CHAPTER 33

One year isn't a long time when an Italian wedding is involved. Preparations consumed Nick and Gina; her parents, Tony and Estelle, and Aunt Mildred, who was invited to take part in the planning.

The venue was selected: La Scala's banquet hall. The wedding singer: Marco Ponzi, rumored to be Tony Bennett's grandnephew. The flowers included roses, sunflowers, tulips, and other delights from northern Italy. Stationery for the invitations was selected in an almost ceremonial meeting with the wedding planner, Jasmine.

The guest list was prepared, revised and finalized. More than 300 were invited: relatives and friends, old country and new, and an assortment of Nick's friends and family, even his uncle coming all the way from Utah.

A wedding website was built. Nick and Gina soon discovered they had friends and followers they'd never met, even a few trolls. Rumor had it that the trolls were prearranged by Jasmine to lend authenticity.

Nick understood his role in the proceedings: sit quietly and approve. He was uncomfortable with the Catholic Mass and its extraordinary trappings, but was assured that a Mormon priest would also be present to co-officiate. All rather civil, Nick thought.

Aunt Mildred continued to write to Carlos about the excitement surrounding the nuptials. Carlos found the website and marked it as a Favorite. He wrote Aunt Mildred, saying he looked forward to attending, reacquainting with family and meeting Nick's friends. Wouldn't miss it for the world.

•　　•　　•　　•　　•

Nick sat in the construction trailer and checked his spreadsheets. Everything on time and within budget. He managed the reduction-in-force needed for the completion of the major tasks, and eliminated staff as evenly as possible from Gallante, Amazon, and Smith. No whiff of partiality.

He knew the Amazons had established a construction headquarters in Hoboken for future Jersey ventures, and that Town Centre was their crown jewel so far. Maurice assured him that an aura of cooperation and professionalism would continue to define the Amazon presence, and he would fight off pressure from company management to force more visibility.

He also met with Luciano when grumbling occurred within the Gallante ranks. Mike Angeloni seemed to be the main thorn in his side. Minor vandalism, slowdowns, wolf whistles, and profanity were reluctantly tolerated as work headed for completion.

The Town Centre civic and business managers took note of Nick's stewardship. The Mormon from Utah, as he was kiddingly, yet respectfully, referred, was a man capable of keeping this amalgam of divided interests on task. He was seen as a rising young star in the South Jersey labor market.

•　　•　　•　　•　　•

A few nights later, Luciano, after one too many beers, shared his increasing concern about losing control of his men, especially Mike Angeloni . Nick, Hank, and Ted listened quietly.

"Guys, it wasn't easy telling you this. There's a code we follow in the community, and we don't air out our dirty laundry. This was something I was reluctant to do, but I don't want a labor war under my watch."

"Thanks, Luciano. This conversation never took place," Ted said.

• • • • •

The flames rose into the late evening sky. Long Harbor Ladder Company 1 was dispatched after a 911 call from a phone booth outside a Wawa blocks away. Hank and Nick were also contacted, as was Chief Hanson.

Two dumpsters spewed fire. The fighters made sure the flames were contained within the metal containers. No adjacent building was affected, except for smoke. The firemen hosed the flames and closed the lids, when safe, to smother the fire. After twenty minutes, everything was declared under control.

Luciano drove up, followed by Maurice. Luciano took in the scene. "Shit," he called out. "Any chance this was an accident?"

The other leaders stood in silence. "We'll collect what evidence we can," said Ted. "If this was intentional, we'll come down hard on whoever did this."

Hank turned to Nick. "Get a crew out here to clean this up once the police release the scene. By tomorrow morning, I want Town Centre back in business. Make it look like nothing happened."

• • • • •

Next morning, Ted drove his cruiser down Lenape Highway, keeping a steady distance from the black Mustang convertible ahead. The driver reached forward and raised the volume on his radio, the vibration and Latin beat prompting stares from passing motorists and pedestrians.

The chief flipped on his siren. Mike Angeloni checked his rearview, seemed to mutter something, and pulled over. Ted waited a few minutes as he called it in, and delayed long enough to anger his prey.

He stopped at the rear of the Mustang. Making sure he was unobserved, he bent down, pulled his flashlight, and tapped the taillight, cracking it. Returning the light to his waistband, he straightened up and walked to the driver-side window.

"Did you know you had a broken taillight, sir? That's a safety violation. License, insurance, and registration, please."

Mike turned in his seat, looking toward the rear of the car. He sighed, pulled his wallet, and handed over the paperwork. "Funny, Officer," he said. "It was OK when I left my apartment."

"It's Chief, young man. Chief of Police Ted Hanson, Long Harbor PD."

Ted looked over the interior of the car, front seat and back, the long examination visibly aggravating his quarry. He focused again on Mike.

"Hey, I've seen you before. You're one of Gallante's men at Town Centre. You guys are doing the plumbing."

"That's right."

"I always marveled at the labor cooperation there," Ted said. "So many workers from such a varied group of tradesmen. Oh, a little vandalism here and there, but generally, peace in the valley."

Ted leaned in. "Did you hear about the fire last night? Two dumpsters in Town Centre near the foreman's trailer. It took a while to contain, but things are good as new now. We're investigating for possible arson. Whoever did this is facing jail time for risking a catastrophe and destruction of property."

Ted stood straight, and flipped open his ticket book. He filled out the violation sheet... slowly. Mike tapped the steering wheel. Ted stopped writing. "Tell you what. You seem like a nice, law-abiding young man. I'll let you off with a warning. Stay out of trouble and get the taillight fixed, Mr. Angeloni."

The chief continued. "Angeloni. A solid name. Someone who takes pride in his community, and walks the straight and narrow. Maybe I'll say hello to you when I drive through Town Centre on my rounds."

"Anything else, Chief?"

"No, Mike, see you around." Ted patted Mike on the shoulder, making him flinch. "Continue toeing the line, young man. The best way to assure a bright and peaceful future ahead."

CHAPTER 34

Hank watered the azaleas in his front yard as Billy Idol blasted from the wireless speaker. Sue pushed the door open, kissed Hank goodbye and started her daily run. Hank watched her disappear down the street.

His cell phone rang, disturbing this moment of peace. *Charlie Benner, hmm.* Hank swiped and held the phone to his ear. "Hank Malone," he announced.

"Hank, this is Charlie. I know you're not with the program anymore, but I just wanted to update you on a status I received from Agent Nelson on our Salt Lake City friends. Bradshaw and Warren are still in Tucson Federal Correctional, 10 years to go, and, not surprisingly, thriving. They even have converts to the Latter-Day Saints." Charlie laughed. "Their men can't knock on cell doors and preach, but, apparently, have other means of influence."

There was a rustle of paper. "Garcia got released on parole almost two years ago, but has been restricted to Utah. That travel limitation is up in June. He still has to check in with authorities, but can go anywhere. Keep a low profile, Hank. He may be looking for you."

"Don't worry, Charlie. I've settled into the suburban life. My biggest worry now is making sure the roses don't shrivel up and die in this ungodly Jersey spring weather." He dodged a honey bee the size of a small drone. "Whoa, Charlie. Even the bees are ferocious here."

"I'm not kidding about Garcia, Hank. Keep flying under the radar until he decides you're not worth looking for."

"Will do, Charlie," Hank said. "Hank Malone is just a boring white-collar Catholic football fan, as far removed from notoriety as you can get."

"Keep it that way, Hank."

CHAPTER 35

Jasmine Lafleur walked into Lenape Casino, spectacular in a pale blue business suit. She nodded to Billy Whitedeer as she strolled by. Men stopped to check out the beauty, their wives walking on, chatting to the airspace that should have held their husbands.

"Jasmine," Billy called out. "A minute?"

She beckoned him over and checked her makeup as Billy wound through the lobby.

"What brings you here today, Jasmine?" He lowered his voice. "I hope you're not soliciting. I'm trying to keep Lenape a good, clean, establishment."

"Don't worry, Billy. I'm working the senior afternoon magic show. Nothing's coming off unless Murray makes it disappear."

"Good to hear. Hey, I heard you're also the wedding planner to the Mancini-Olsen wedding. I'll be there tomorrow."

"Small world, Billy. Maybe I'll see you."

Billy walked over to greet guests, as Jasmine found the Warrior night club and, adjusting her skirt for a second, walked in.

"Jasmine, just in time," said Murray the Magnificent. "The bus tour is chowing down at the buffet. They'll file in for the magic show in about 15 minutes."

She brushed a feather from Murray's coat. "Murray, you know, we make quite a team. A black transvestite model in a blonde wig, and a bald tuxedoed illusionist."

Murray grinned. "Beauty and the Beast, I'd say." He shook his wand, and plastic flowers appeared. He handed them to his chanteuse, who sniffed them like they were real. "Everything's an illusion, anyway, isn't it?" Murray said.

"'Everything is show biz', as they sing in *The Producers*," Jasmine said. "As long as we make a lasting impression. What am I singing today?"

"*There's No Business Like Show Business* to start. Then a few from *The Music Man,* and we finish with *Gentlemen Prefer Blondes.*"

"Perfect, Murray. Maybe someone will discover me and want to use my talents."

Murray laughed. "You're a renaissance woman, Jasmine. Wedding planner, singer, actress, God knows what else. What man, or woman, could resist you?"

• • • • •

Hank sat in Starbucks nursing his latte and picking at the lemon cake. Friday afternoon, the day before Nick and Gina's wedding. He took the day off to pick up his tux, buy a wedding gift for the couple, and enjoy some quiet time as Sue and Gina met for manicures, pedicures, facials, and whatever else women did at these moments.

Guys are more laid back. No real physical preparation needed. Make sure the tux fits, clean underwear, maybe a hair trim. That's it. He sat back and observed his café mates, mostly college kids, red hat society matrons, aspiring novelists typing at laptops hoping to become the next Hemingway or Sylvia Plath. He couldn't hear conversations, nor did he want to, the ambient noise of chatter, laughter, and espresso machines providing a soothing background for his midday meal.

A man in a Hawaiian shirt barely containing his frame walked to the counter accompanied by a pert brunette. He studied the menu. "What's the difference between a Tall, Grande and Venti?" he asked, his voice resonating.

The barista stood straight, her chance to educate a client on coffee house Italian. "Tall is a twelve ounce, Grande is sixteen, and Venti, of course, is twenty."

"Of course," said the man. "I'll have ... hmm ... a Very Berry Hibiscus Lemonade. Make it a Grande. To go"

He turned to the woman. "I'll have a Mango Dragonfruit Lemonade," she said. "The largest you got."

Hank raised his head. *Where do I know that voice from?* He shrugged and resumed eating his cake.

"Can I have a name for your order, sir?" the barista said after entering the information into the terminal.

"Yes," the man said, raising his voice louder. "The name is Louie. Louie the Ferret."

Hank fumbled his fork and turned. Carlos smiled back. Hank stood and hurried toward the door. Candy stepped in his path and hugged her former lover. "Hi. It's been a long time, Louie."

He returned to his table, sat, and sighed as Carlos and Candy walked over. Carlos pulled a chair from the next table, Candy sat opposite. Carlos laughed. "Well, of all the gin joints in all the towns in all the world, we walk into his."

Candy studied Hank's face. "I have to say, Louie. They did a good job on you. Straightened out the prominent lines, worked on the eyebrows, and generally turned you into someone you're not."

"This *is* who I am, Candy. Hank Malone, proud citizen of Long Harbor, New Jersey. Thousands of miles and years from my past."

"And yet, here we are," said Carlos. "Did Nick tell you I was his Uncle?"

"Shit," said Hank, unable to think of anything better. "Are you here to kill me?"

Carlos looked around quickly, making sure that last remark wasn't noted. "I'm not sure yet, Louie ... or Hank, whoever you are now. It would probably put a damper on Nick's wedding. Can't have the best man found floating in the harbor."

"Louie the Ferret," called the barista, drawing stares from most people in the shop.

Carlos raised his hand. "Right here. I'll be over in a sec."

Candy grabbed her purse and stood. Carlos leaned on the table. "Don't leave town, Louie. I have locals following you and watching your house. We'll sit down after the wedding and see what we can work out.

There's quite a price on your head. Right now, everyone in Salt Lake City thinks I'm attending my nephew's wedding. I didn't tell them about you."

He stood. "I wanted to make sure it really *was* Louie Kimball. Now, I can let them know, or maybe we can work out a deal ourselves. In the meantime, think about where you can come up with lots of money in the next few days. Two hundred grand sounds about right."

He turned and walked to the drink counter. Candy picked up a napkin and dabbed Hank's face, removing latte foam from his upper lip. "See you around, lover."

●　　●　　●　　●　　●

Hank sat in his car and slammed the steering wheel. He checked his mirrors. *Is anyone trailing me? Maybe I should call Charlie and ask to be reinstated.* He banged his head on the headrest. *No, can't do that. He'd have me out of here in a second. Gotta think this through.*

He drove home, checking for any car following. *Nothing there. Maybe Carlos was bluffing.* Pulling into his driveway, he saw three men in white shirts and black pants holding glossy leaflets. *Are they waiting for me? This can't be my tail.*

He left his car and walked up to the men. "Hi, gentlemen. Let me guess, Latter-Day Saints. Come in, come in, and take a load off."

"You're too kind, sir. Normally we don't get such a reception."

He pointed them to a couch and brought out cookies and bottled water. "Tell me, gentlemen. How'd you end up in South Jersey? I thought you were all from Utah and out West."

"I'm Elder Ethen Romney." Hank opened his mouth but Ethen shook his finger. "No, I'm not part of *those* Romneys. At least not a close relative." He gestured to his companions. "These are Elders Evans and Nielsen."

Hank toast back and looked at the three. "And you're from Jersey?"

"Yes, we are. We preach out of the Camden meeting house. Maybe you know Vai Olamalu, the former football player. One of the spiritual leaders. A credit to our community."

I'm a Predators fan myself," said Hank, "But it's interesting to learn how you were able to establish your church in such nontraditional territory."

"Well, Mr. Malone, it took hard work, dedication to duty, and … ," he pointed to the soles of his loafers, "plenty of shoe leather."

"How did you know my name?"

Elder Romney frowned. "Leader Garcia told us to be careful with you. Lesson learned." He stood with his two companions. "Have a great day, Mr. Malone." He smiled. "And as they say in the police shows, don't leave town." He signaled to his men. "We'll see ourselves out."

The men left as Hank sipped his water and thought. A minute later he walked out the front door and stood on the front porch looking for them at neighboring houses. No sign. Sue's Camry pulled into the driveway. She signaled Hank over and handed him a bag of groceries as she opened the door and got out. "What's up, Hank? Were you getting some fresh air?"

"Yeah." Hank scratched his nose.

They both stood silent for a few awkward seconds. "OK, Hank. Spill it."

"Did you see three men, white shirts, dark pants, walking down the street?"

"No, Hank. Missionaries again?"

Hank was silent.

"Shit, Hank. Did they come for you?"

●　　●　　●　　●　　●

They discussed their options. Telling the FBI and running away in the middle of the night was the last resort. It meant the end to a life they had built together. Skipping the wedding wasn't an option, either. Spoiling the day for their best friends and disappointing family was too much. There had to be another option.

Hank ran an idea through Sue. She agreed, but doubted the wisdom. Not many choices available, though. He called Nick. "Hey, Nick, I have a favor to ask. I have friends in town and I'd like to invite them to the wedding. Is that OK?"

"Sure, Hank. We have a few last-minute regrets so your friends can come. I'll just modify the place cards. Who are they?"

"Mr. Charles Benner and his uncle, Sidney Baker."

*   *   *   *   *

Hank called Charlie and told of his encounter with Carlos. The FBI agent suggested leaving immediately, but Hank declined and detailed his alternative. Sid Baker was conferenced in. He liked the idea. Charlie went along and offered to meet with Sid and Hank. Hank declined; people were watching him.

Charlie opened his closet to find a dark suit for the wedding. He had 20 of them, so no problem there. He focused on the tie. Nothing G-man, something lighthearted but appropriate.

Later on, Charlie met Sid in Starbucks. His boss was upbeat. "This could be fun," he said. "Observing the enemy out in the open. We'll see where this can go with Garcia and decide what to do with our visitor. Who knows, if we play this right, we can land bigger fish."

Sid noticed a beautiful twenty something two tables over, laboring over a laptop and sipping a macchiato. He went to the counter, bought a packet of biscotti, and walked over to the young lady. Charlie watched as she started to recoil at the approach, but then warmed to her visitor.

The bureau chief chatted with her for a few minutes, stood, bowed slightly, whispered something that made her laugh, and walked back to Charlie's table. "Nice young lady," he said. "She loved my story about being caught outside my dorm in the middle of winter with only a toga on."

"That's my story, darn it, Sid," Charlie said, shaking his head.

"Yeah, but Uncle Sidney can tell it better. I still got it, Charlie. I'll have people eating out of my hand." He laughed. "I know what to do now. And poor Garcia won't suspect anything."

CHAPTER 36

The sun arose on the spectacular, cloudless June day, promising a bright afternoon. St. Augustine's Church was a beehive of delivery men, decorators, and choir members rehearsing. Tony and Estelle arranged for the whole chorus to perform, promising a sizeable donation to the building fund, and invitations to the reception.

Father Theo sat on the edge of a pew and engaged Jasmine, the wedding planner, in small talk. He pointed to architectural highlights in the ceiling and walls of this small but old parish church, while sneaking the occasional glance at her cleavage.

Jasmine fluttered her eyelashes as Theo detailed the highlights of his house of worship. She crossed her legs, Theo swallowing his gum, and coughed.

Tony walked in and winked at Jasmine. He asked Theo for a few minutes of his time. The men walked to the sacristy as the wedding planner checked the streamers and lighting. "So, Father, the church is beautiful, the choir is practicing, and Jasmine is taking care of the last details. This should be a fun day."

"The Lord always embraces couples and welcomes their family and guests to the celebration of matrimony. It's joyous to all," Theo said.

"Good." Tony reached into his pocket and removed an envelope. "And here's something for your participation, Father. Get yourself something nice."

Theo examined the contents and gasped. "The church welcomes your generosity, Mr. Mancini. The money will be put to good use."

Tony leaned forward and whispered. "There's enough there for a set of woods, Theo. The Lord will understand if you spend a little on yourself."

"I'll put it to good use, Tony."

The father of the bride turned to admire the decorations. Jasmine smiled and walked toward the men. "You know, Theo. Jasmine is a transvestite." He sniffed his boutonniere. "I bet others today will make the same mistake you made. Buy those clubs and forget about pleasures of the flesh." He laughed. "Especially these days, when you need a program to tell which plumbing is attached."

Theo studied Jasmine from a distance. "Point taken, Tony. There's a lot less harm on the golf course."

●   ●   ●   ●   ●

Hank checked his tux in the mirror as Sue examined her gown. "Man, we've only been married a few years and already clothes don't fit us like they used to," Hank said.

She turned to her husband. "Speak for yourself, Malone. I still turn heads in the hospital corridor."

He started to respond, then decided to let things lie. "I'm glad Theo let us change here," he said, glancing out the window of the church office room. "It must be 90 out there. Flop sweating in a monkey suit is the last thing I need."

A silver Acura convertible pulled into the lot. Carlos made sure to use two parking spots, jumped out, and opened the passenger door for Candy. Hank's former lover swung her legs around and took Carlos's hand, adjusting her red dress as she stood.

Her red-carpet arrival was observed by male guests, and an altar boy who crashed his Schwinn into the bike rack. Carlos and Candy hurried over and helped the boy to his feet. He brushed off his clothes, took one last look, then hurried to the sacristy door.

Carlos whispered something to Candy, who laughed. They started for the front entrance of St. Augustine's. Hank saw Nick hurry out of the reflection garden and call to Carlos, who stopped, shook Nick's hand, and gestured to Candy, who hugged Nick.

"One big happy family," Hank whispered.

Sue walked over and watched the reunion. "Is that Carlos, Hank?"

"Yeah. And the old friend from Vegas I mentioned."

"Wow, Hank. She's a knockout. It must have been hard to leave her."

"Louie left her, Sue," Hank said. "Hank's a happily married man."

• • • • •

The groomsmen: Hank, Ted, and Billy Whitedeer, met Nick, Father Theo, and High Priest Spence Allred. Hank studied the men. *A fugitive in witness protection, a police chief, a Lenape Indian, an LDS elder, a hippie Catholic priest, and a tall, thin Mormon High Priest. We resemble a modern-day Village People.*

Theo and Spence went over the ceremony, repeating the gist of the prior night's rehearsal. Ted would lead, followed by Billy, then Hank, and finally Nick. They'll stand at the foot of the altar. Theo and Spence will follow with the altar boys and stand at the top of the steps. The men will await the bridal party. The bridesmaids come up, one at a time. Gina will walk up the aisle last with Tony, who will kiss her, shake Nick's hand, and join Estelle in the front pew.

Ted, Billy, Hank, and Nick walked to the altar area. They positioned themselves and awaited the bridesmaids. Hank observed the guests, dressed in fine clothes and whispering. He searched for a red dress. Not too many. Finally, he saw Candy chatting with Carlos. She made eye contact with Hank and emitted that killer smile that used to make Louie melt. She licked her lips. Hank closed his eyes and thought of the Predators scoring a winning TD. *That's better. Gotta stay focused.*

Pachelbel's Canon in D began as the assembled turned to the entrance. Gina and Tony started the walk down the aisle, the white runner carpet leading the way. Nick beamed as he met Gina's gaze. Tony kept to the traditional serious pose of a father about to lose his daughter.

At the altar, Tony lifted Gina's veil and kissed her on the cheek. He stepped over to Nick and pumped his hand. "Take care of my daughter," he whispered.

Nick nodded. "I will." He joined Gina before Father Theo and High Priest Spence, while Tony sat next to Estelle, who was sobbing.

Hank noticed Carlos. The large man was dabbing his eyes while Candy patted his shoulder. *A loving uncle and extortionist. Ready to congratulate the happy couple before he shakes down the Best Man.*

Charlie Benner sat in one of the rear aisles. The agent was stoic and somewhat distracted by Sid Baker, his boss, who was taking photos of the ceremony while also turning the camera on himself and Charlie for selfies.

●   ●   ●   ●   ●

Theo and Spence performed like they'd done this for years. They alternated Bible readings, and both gave quick, funny sermons, seeming to enjoy each other and the proceedings, while keeping the focus on Nick and Gina.

They uttered a simultaneous, 'I now pronounce you husband and wife,' gestured to Nick to kiss his bride, and led the assembly in a generous round of applause. The couple kissed, left the altar, and strolled down the aisle as guests took photos.

Uncle Sidney stepped out of the pew and took a panorama, capturing the lovely couple, while also getting a good frontal view of Carlos and Candy.

The line of well-wishers greeted the couple at the entrance to the church. When the FBI agents were next, Hank stepped forward. "Nick and Gina, these are my friends Charlie and Sidney. They're visiting and I asked Nick if they could come."

Nick shook hands with each. "It's a pleasure to meet you. Thanks for coming."

"We're thrilled to be here and happy for both of you," Sid said. "Hank was so looking forward to this day and excited for the chance to share it with us."

The men returned to their car. As they climbed in, Sid texted the panorama to the Salt Lake City FBI office, promising more closeups of the Utah visitors. The silver Acura convertible sped by, salsa music blasting from the speaker. Sid laughed. "Uncle Sidney needs to meet that pair, Charley. They seem like a fun couple."

CHAPTER 37

The La Scala banquet hall started to fill. The slow, flickering lights and red and white color scheme resembled an Italian bistro in early evening, the stars winking their welcome. Guests found their tables, laid suit coats and wraps over chairs, then wandered to the open bar.

Tony checked with Jasmine: all in order. The former semipro football player, now fabulous in sequined gown, handed him a mimosa. "Leave everything to me, Mr. Mancini. Enjoy your daughter and son-in-law's reception."

Tony took a sip of the orange juice and champagne drink. "Jasmine, this is perfect, and just the right temperature." He laughed. "Marry me."

The wedding planner shook her head. "I'm flattered, Tony, but save yourself for Estelle." She gestured toward the entranceway. "Besides, I have my eye on that dashing man in the pastel suit and bow tie."

"Ah, that's Hank Malone's buddy Sid, a late addition to the wedding." He finished his drink. "I do say, he doesn't waste any time. He's already chatting up that gorgeous woman in the red dress."

"I'd be careful if I was him," Jasmine said. "Her boyfriend is big and mean looking."

"That's Nick's Uncle Carlos from Utah. Cried like a baby during the ceremony, but I'm guessing it wouldn't pay to cross him."

Carlos and Candy laughed at something Sid said. Sid leaned in, at close range to Candy's cleavage, and positioned his camera for a selfie. The three said 'cheese' loud enough to have other guests turn around.

"And that's Sid's friend Charlie in the background," Tony noted. "More staid than his friend, but cheerful. I'm guessing he and Sid are like the "Wedding Crashers," unknown to either bride or groom, but soon to be the life of the party."

•　　•　　•　　•　　•

Charlie found their table while Sid checked the pictures of his new friends. He texted the clearest photo to Agent Nelson, captioning the picture, "Our mutual acquaintances."

Sue walked over, cleared her throat, and smiled at the pair. "Hi, I'm Hank's wife, Sue. Sid and Charlie, Hank speaks highly of you. It's so good you could come."

Sid pulled out a chair and dusted it with his napkin. "It's our pleasure, Mrs. Malone. We and Hank go way back."

Sue opened her bag, pulled a cosmetic mirror and checked herself. "I hope you guys know what you're doing."

Sid laughed loud enough to make others stop talking and look over. "Don't worry, Mrs. Malone. Leave everything to your Uncle Sid."

Hank walked over and placed his hand on Sue's shoulder. "Now, Sue, you can chat later with our friends. They want us to get ready for the introduction of the bridal party."

As the couple left, Charlie turned to Sid. "Is she going to be a problem?"

"Maybe," said Sid. "But let's stick to the plan."

•　　•　　•　　•　　•

Hank tapped his champagne glass. Some chatting continued until Jasmine tapped her own glass and gave the evil eye to the few who continued to talk. Hank cleared his throat.

"Nick, Gina, we're all excited and honored to be here on this special day. I met Nick just a few years ago and quickly understood how special he was. A good, clean-living man, of strong faith, conviction and moral character. He wasn't a Predator fan then, but with time, patience, and strong-armed tactics, he saw the light."

Hank turned to the bride. "Then he met Gina: great cook, loving person, and passionate about life. This was a match made in heaven. Nick and Gina, you are starting ..."

He stopped at the sound of loud sobbing. Carlos was blubbering into his napkin. "Nick and Gina, you are starting..." A honk resonated through the room as Carlos blew his nose into the same piece of linen.

Jasmine hurried over with a new napkin. Holding the used cloth at arm's length, she handed it to a busboy for disposal.

"Nick and Gina, you are starting a new life together, surrounded by friends and family. We all wish you the best in the years, even decades, to come. Remember that the journey may be tough at times, sometimes you may just want to leave town and start over."

He glanced at Carlos. "But you can't run from your problems and your responsibilities." Nick and Gina frowned and looked at each other. "You must meet life head-on and know that in the end, through love, understanding, and friends, all will work out. Carpe Diem."

He turned to the guests. "So, ladies and gentlemen, please lift your glasses and salute Nick and Gina, a first-class couple and a credit to Long Harbor, their families, and friends. May they have many years of happiness together."

The guests drank, even the Mormons who took polite sips. The guests then tapped their glasses, signaling that the couple should kiss. Nick and Gina obliged.

Carlos started blubbering again. Sidney walked up the center row and took a picture of the newly wedded couple, then turned to the crowd. "OK, everyone, Cheeeeessssssseeee."

The guests obliged as Sid shot away. "Perfect." He then returned to his table and showed the photos to Charlie, who appeared to be embarrassed.

Jasmine stepped forward. "OK, everyone. Dinner will be served soon. I hope you're hungry." With that, waitstaff marched out of the kitchen, holding silver trays. Servers made sure champagne and water glasses were refilled. Small talk resumed. Hank sat and chatted with Sue. Sid and Charlie lined up guests at each table for selfies. Sid was part of every picture.

●　　　●　　　●　　　●　　　●

Marco Ponzi took the microphone. "Ok, folks, when in La Scala, do as the Italians do. Please join Nick and Gina on the dance floor as we take you to Venice." He started to sing *That's Amore*. Couples followed the pair to the wooden marquee floor. Sid bowed to Jasmine and asked for a dance. She took his hand and followed him.

Jasmine led with Sid following, mostly backpedaling. "So, how's my favorite FBI Bureau chief?" she said. "I haven't seen you in ages."

"Good, Jasmine. How's the bureau's favorite informant? You seem to have found your niche here."

"I loooovvvvvee this job," Jasmine said. "People are always excited about the occasion, but need that little touch of elegance that I provide."

"You're not *selling*, I hope."

"Only dreams and happiness. Don't need a supplier for that."

Jasmine dipped Sid, who could have been mistaken for Ginger Rogers at that moment. She lifted her partner gently, then allowed him to take the lead as they performed a basket whip.

"So, Jasmine, do you think you have it all down? Can you sell it? Like I said, it's worth a thousand to you if everything goes right. Not bad for a night's work."

He detailed the plan again as they moved to *O Sole Mio*.

"Sid, it's a brilliant idea. And easy money for an actress such as me." She laughed. "And here he comes."

Sid felt a tap on his shoulder. Carlos motioned that he wanted to cut in. He yielded and Carlos swarmed Jasmine like a prizefighter trying to make it to the final bell. The bureau chief bowed to Jasmine and walked off to rejoin Charlie at the table. His friend was plowing into a piece of tiramisu.

Another tap. "Can I have this dance?"

Sid took Candy into his arms as *O Sole Mio* finished. Sid smiled at Candy, awaiting the next song.

"And now folks, in honor of the lovely couple, and Gina's strict Italian upbringing, I sing to you a nice ballad," Marco said as the band started. A murmur rose as the guests recognized the tune. The floor filled.

Marco started to sing, "When I was a boy, just about-a eighth-a grade." People started singing, mostly men. When the chorus arrived with *Whatsa Matta You*, everyone joined in. Sid started to jitterbug. She kept up, never missing a beat. When *Shaddup You Face* finished, the guests shouted and applauded. Sid bowed to Candy and escorted her back to her table. He turned to find Carlos breathing heavily. "What a woman," Carlos said. "They don't make 'em like that in Utah."

Sid glanced over at Jasmine, who was adjusting her dress. "No, I guess they don't."

Candy gestured at Sid. "He's quite a dancer, Carlos, and apparently an old friend of Hank's."

Sid grinned. "He jokingly calls me Uncle Sid. We're both Predator fans." He winked at Candy. "There's nothing like swooping in on unsuspecting prey."

• • • • •

Hank watched Sid as he worked his magic. He nudged Sue. "Uncle Sid's a big hit. Leave it all to him."

"He looks like he's about to steal Carlos's girlfriend."

"Carlos appears to be smitten with Jasmine, the wedding planner."

"He doesn't know she's a transvestite?"

"Doesn't look like it. There weren't too many in Salt Lake City."

Nick and Gina walked over. "Your Uncle Sid is the life of the party, Hank," Gina said. "It's always good to have someone like that at a reception."

Hank looked toward Sid, who was now twisting with the flower girl. "My uncle always saves the day. It's never a dull moment with him."

CHAPTER 38

The reception was winding down. The cake was cut, the bridal bouquet caught by Mona, Gina's sister. Sid caught the garter after Charlie reacted to a shot in the ribs as he was about to snatch it midair.

Hank watched as Sid walked over to Candy's table, bowed, bent over and slid the garter up her ankle. Candy lifted her knee to admire the fit. Sid stood, whispered in her ear, and the couple were off to parts unknown.

Sue pulled at Hank's arm as Marco started to sing *Moon River*. The pair walked to the dance floor, embraced, and moved to the music. Nick and Gina joined in, as well as Tony and Estelle. Charlie walked up also, leading Mona.

"This has been the perfect day," Gina said to Nick and Hank. "People happy, dancing, eating, and having a great time."

Hank looked around for Carlos. The big man was chatting up Jasmine.

Love appears to be in the air," Sue said. "Charlie and Mona are hitting it off, Uncle Sid and Candy seem to be enjoying each other's company, and Nick's Uncle Carlos is schmoozing Jasmine."

Nick studied the pair. "Isn't Jasmine a ...".

"Now, don't judge, Nick," said Hank, suppressing a laugh. "We all need to make it through the night."

●   ●   ●   ●   ●

Hank and Sue got home around 11:30 p.m. "We used to stay out until two a.m.," Sue said. "Now we rarely make it past *The Late Show*."

"We can't keep up anymore, Sue," said Hank. "I didn't even know half of the music at the reception. I figured Marco would cater to the thirty-somethings and the baby boomers, but he knew and sang a lot of the current stuff." He laughed. "Maybe we missed the boat on modern tastes."

Sue flopped into the Lazy Boy and kicked off her heels, barely missing Hank as he reached for the remote. Hank picked up a shoe and examined it. "Not orthopedic, so maybe we're still alive and kicking."

"So, Hank. Is Carlos going to rat us out, uproot our lives, and disturb the peace?"

"I saw Charlie at the end of the reception. He says he and Sid have a plan for Carlos."

"And don't forget Candy. Although, Sid seems to have her complete attention for now."

"Good old Uncle Sidney," laughed Hank. "Legendary in local FBI lure. I now understand his appeal."

"So, we just wait to hear from the FBI and hope for the best?"

"Do you want to pick up and run?" Hank asked.

"I couldn't run anywhere at the moment. Maybe staying put is the best approach."

"I agree, Sue. Anyway, I hear Carlos is still technically on parole, so he has to be careful how he sees this through. Let's leave things to Sid and Charlie."

●   ●   ●   ●   ●

Carlos drove Jasmine to his hotel, jumped out and opened her door. She slid out and winked at the smitten man. Carlos reached into the back seat and grabbed two small bottles of champagne. He read the label: *Nick and Gina, Two Together*. He handed them to Jasmine.

"Let me find my key, make sure Candy and her date haven't beaten us to the room, and get a bucket of ice. I'm in 221, come up in five minutes."

"See you then." She waited for Carlos to get out of sight, texted "221" to Charlie, unscrewed a bottle, dropped in a sedative and swirled the contents.

Finding the room, she turned the door handle. Unlocked. Carlos was on the bed, stripped down to his striped boxers and white T-shirt, *The Killers* playing in the background.

"Not too many Mormon rock bands, but these guys can really tune it up."

Jasmine found two plastic glasses. She poured half of the spiked bottle into one, and opened the other, pouring one for herself and emptying the rest into the sink. She carried the spiked bottle and the glasses to Carlos's bedside. She handed him a glass and held hers out for a toast. "To us," she said.

"To us," Carlos said, emptying the contents. Jasmine refilled his glass.

"I have to tell you, you throw quite a party, Jasmine. Good food and drink, good music, and even a few surprises."

"The night is young, Carlos. More surprises to come."

"I can't wait," the big man said. "Seems like Candy found her Prince Charming for the evening. So, it's just you and me."

She raised her glass to Carlos. "Here's to finding *my* Prince Charming."

●   ●   ●   ●   ●

Charlie parked his government-issued Ford Taurus at a Walgreens, a block from the hotel occupied by Carlos and Jasmine. "Why are we stopping here, Charlie?" Mona said. "I thought we were going to my apartment."

"I need to pick up a few things, sweetie. Be right out."

Mona grinned. "Gotcha, Charlie. Hurry up."

Charlie smiled. "Believe me, Mona. I can't wait."

Mona giggled and opened her bottle of champagne.

He walked into the almost empty drug store. The only employee he could see was stocking shelves in the back. Charlie took note of the outside surveillance cameras. "That one on the left should have captured Carlos and his paramour," he whispered. "Informant, transvestite, felon. How will that play in Salt Lake City, Mr. Garcia?"

He selected a box of condoms and signaled the clerk, who put down a case of Motrin and hurried up front. "Have a good evening, sir," the man said, handing Charlie the receipt.

Charlie laughed. "Oh, I'm sure this evening will be epic."

CHAPTER 39

Birds chirped and squirrels skittered up the maple tree outside Room 221. Jasmine checked her phone clock: 7 a.m., time for the photo session with Charlie. She spooned herself into Carlos's back, waiting for the big man to wake up. He awoke and turned to her. "Good morning. Boy, I must have been tired. I don't remember too much."

"You were wonderful, you big, gentle giant. Better than I imagined."

Jasmine removed the sheet, exposing her male equipment. "Now let me do you."

Carlos hurried out of bed, put on his glasses, and gasped. "Is this some sort of prank?"

"No lover, just two lost souls finding each other."

Carlos slid on his pants, grabbed his car keys, and ran from the room. Jasmine stood at the open door, naked and shivering from the morning breeze. She waited a minute, assuming that was all Charlie needed to capture the scene. She called out to Carlos, who was starting the Acura. "Come back, honeybunch." Carlos sped off.

· · · · ·

Charlie drove to a Wawa and picked up two coffees, burritos, and a newspaper. He drove to Mona's apartment, blared the horn and carried his treasure to the front door. Unlocked. Dropping the items onto the dining room table, he walked into the bedroom and climbed into bed. "I thought maybe you left," Mona said.

"Never, my love. Just picking us up something for breakfast. I hope you're hungry."

"Famished," Mona said. "How's the weather outside?"

"A bright, sunny, beautiful day. Full of promise and surprises."

•   •   •   •   •

Sid answered his phone as Candy turned and started snoring again. He stood and walked to the motel door. "Hello. Charlie, talk to me." He covered his mouth to avoid waking Candy.

"So far, so good, Sid. I have Nelson doing his part in Salt Lake City," Charlie said. "After today, our friend won't want to be anywhere near Utah."

Candy awakened. She patted the bed and motioned to Sid. "Gotta go now, Charlie. Catch you later."

•   •   •   •   •

Candy's cell rang. She grabbed a sheet and walked over to the table, holding the charged phone. Sid walked to the night table and refilled their champagne glasses. Cindy gave him a thumbs-up.

"Hello, Carlos?"

Frantic words. "You have to talk slower," she said. More panicked, rapid-paced talking, loud enough for Sid to catch the urgency. "You say Jasmine has a trick?"

More words. Candy covered her mouth to mask her laughter. "Wait a minute. Jasmine is a man? How long did it take to figure *that* out?"

Silence, then lower volume as Carlos appeared to catch his breath. "You may have been drugged? Champagne? I don't know, Carlos, ours was fine."

She held the phone away as Carlos shouted on his end. "Where am I?" Candy repeated. "I'm in Sid's room at the Sea Breeze." She laughed. "Sid has one, too, although I don't think it's like your problem. Where are you now?"

Candy found a pen and wrote on a notepad. "The Starbucks on Ocean and 9th." She paused, tapping the pen on the Formica table. "I need to do a few things, Carlos, but can meet you there in an hour." A shout, then an apparent obscenity. "I *said* in an hour, Carlos. I have a few things to take care of." She hung up as Carlos continued to plead with her.

She walked to the bed, dropped her sheet, and climbed in. "You'll never guess what happened to Carlos." She laughed. "I don't think he'll ever forget his trip to New Jersey."

●　　　●　　　●　　　●　　　●

The Starbucks buzzed with customers on the late Sunday morning. Carlos found a couch and glared people away from the seat next to him. He sipped a macchiato, bit into a cheese Danish, and checked his phone. No love note from Jasmine. *Why did I give her my number last night?*

Candy walked in, followed by Sid. Seeing Carlos, they nodded and walked over as the man slumped down. When they reached the sofa, Candy wagged a finger. "Remember Carlos, always check the equipment before you buy."

The big man grunted. "This is embarrassing. I hope I didn't catch anything."

Sid sat next to him. "I wouldn't worry about that, my man. Jasmine is very careful. In and out and she's done. Never knew what hit you."

"So, you knew he was ..."

"A transvestite? Of course. Everyone there knew ... well, *almost.*" Sid laughed. "Gina's father told me he had to warn off Father Theo. *That* would have been a real scandal."

Carlos sat up. "We gotta get out of this town before everyone finds out. We'll deal with our other matter later."

Sid slid closer. "That would be Louie Kimball, I gather." He reached into his pocket and removed his badge. "Sid Baker, FBI, Philadelphia bureau."

Carlos slumped as Sid continued. "So, Candy and I had a little heart to heart. She admitted to your plan and agreed to cooperate. We'll let her off with only being a bad judge of character. You, my friend, are in deep. Extortion can put you back behind bars for a long time."

He made a gesture framing Carlos in a pretend camera. "Plus, we have pictures of Jasmine waving you goodbye, naked as the day she was born, as you ran out of the hotel. Not a crime, necessarily, but, I'm sure, embarrassing to an elder. We sent the pictures to the Salt Lake City office ... for identification purposes, of course."

Sid glanced at Carlos's macchiato. "Looks like you need a refill, Carlos. Let me get you one. Need anything, Candy?"

"A Grande espresso. Oh, and a biscotti."

"Isn't she adorable, Carlos? She'll get used to Jersey in no time."

Sid stood, reached for his MasterCard, and shook it at Carlos. "Didn't leave home without it. Good for entertaining customers." He leaned on the table, face to face with him. "My partner Charlie is outside. Don't even think of leaving."

●　　●　　●　　●　　●

Hank and Sue walked in after greeting Charlie, who was standing outside, sipping a strawberry Frappuccino. They saw Carlos first, sitting with Candy. The man seemed a little pale, drumming his fingers. Candy pointed to the counter. Sid was deciphering the menu and joking with the teenager operating the register.

Hank stood in line behind Sid, unsure whether to greet him. The bureau chief turned. "Hank ... and your lovely wife, Sue. This is perfect. I was going to call you later. Candy and I were just having breakfast with Nick's Uncle Carlos. Small world, huh?"

He gave his name and credit card to the barista and pointed to Hank. "And put what they're having on my plastic."

He gestured to Candy and Carlos. "We'll make some room for you. It will be like an intimate wedding afterparty."

• • • • •

Hank and Sue sat on the couch across from Candy and Carlos, as Sid pulled up a chair and faced both couples. "Hank and Sue, did you know Jasmine was a transvestite?"

Sue laughed. "Of course, everyone knows that. That's why he makes such a great party planner. He's our own RuPaul."

Sid took a sip of his coffee. "Well, our friend Carlos was unaware." He chuckled. "Until his personal drag race this morning." He signaled Charlie to join them. "You should see the picture of him running out of the hotel room, buckling his pants with one hand as he unlocks his car with the other. A real classic."

Charlie came in, dropped his cup into the trash, and walked to the table.

"Tell us about Carlos's bad day, Charlie," Sid said. "I already mentioned the photo session."

"Well, the FBI office in Salt Lake City was delighted with the pictures. Copies are posted up in the break room and sent to our contacts in the LDS. The bureau also knows about your extortion plot and is preparing new charges." Charlie pulled up a chair and sat. "So, Carlos. You're up the creek without a paddle. You can't go back to Utah, you're facing new jail time, and, generally, you're screwed."

Sid crushed his coffee cup. "There is one way out, my friend. Tell us whatever you know about corruption that didn't come out in trial: names, dates, activities. If we can make any of it stick, we'll call off Salt Lake City and make you disappear ... witness protection like your former associate."

Carlos groaned.

"We'll send you away to somewhere quiet and peaceful." He leaned in. "Ever been to Kentucky?"

The group walked out of the shop, with Charlie handcuffing Carlos, stuffing him into the back seat, and driving off. Sid shrugged to Candy,

Hank, and Sue. His cell rang, and he walked over to another table. "Baker," he answered.

Hank turned to Candy. "Well, I'm guessing Sid's your knight in shining armor, ready to defend his damsel against all possible attackers."

Candy smoothed her dress. "It sure seems that way, Louie, er, Hank. I guess if we wait long enough good things happen." She turned to Sue. "Looks like you found a good one yourself."

"She's a good one, indeed, Candy. Though I think she'd be more of a threat to an approaching dragon than I would be. It's funny how things turn out."

CHAPTER 40

As Gina packed for the Las Vegas honeymoon, Nick called the Days Inn. The front desk clerk reported that Mr. Garcia and Ms. Hastings had checked out earlier. "Are you sure," he asked. "I'm his nephew. We planned to meet today."

"We're certain, sir. There was quite a crew helping them pack." The clerk lowered his voice. "Is Mr. Garcia a celebrity? Our guests don't usually draw this amount of attention."

"No. Just a normal Joe from Utah," Nick said, thinking this over. "Maybe he had to leave on urgent business."

"Not to talk out of school, Sir, but his girlfriend left with another man." He sighed. "But it's really none of my business. Just another day at Days Inn, I guess."

Nick hung up, thought a minute, and called Aunt Mildred. "No, dear. I hadn't heard anything," she said. "And here I was, planning a quick lunch for Carlos, his girlfriend, Hank, and Sue Malone, and you and Gina, before you flew to Vegas and Carlos went back to Salt Lake City." Mildred sighed. "And, darn it, I made some nice potato salad and iced tea."

"We'll still stop by, Aunt Mildred. Maybe Uncle Carlos had to take an earlier flight."

"OK, Nicky, See you and your lovely bride soon."

• • • • •

Hank and Sue had already arrived when Nick and Gina pulled up. As the newly wedded couple approached the front step, the door opened. Mildred was beaming, Hank and Sue cheering them. They stepped over the threshold, Gina balancing a plate of cannolis.

Nick peered into the living room and laughed. "Where's your Uncle Sid, Hank?" he asked. "I half expected him to greet us, too. He seemed to be everywhere yesterday."

"He had to go into work today," Hank said. "The man is a workaholic."

Mildred took the tray from Gina. "Let me take those, dear. I'll put them in the fridge for dessert. I made hoagies, potato salad, an ambrosia salad, homemade lemonade, and iced tea." Mildred patted Nick's arm. "Your Uncle Carlos doesn't know what he missed."

• • • • •

Carlos sat in Interrogation Suite A in the FBI's Center City, Philadelphia, office. He bit into his sliced turkey sandwich, shoveled in a spoonful of mac and cheese, and sipped a Dr. Pepper. Footsteps passed by the barred window of the small basement room.

Sid walked in, carrying a bag of Cheetos. He laid a paper napkin on the table, poured most of the bag onto it, took a few, and sat across from him. "Lucky we're next door to a Wawa. Hard to get a quick sandwich early on a Sunday afternoon."

He licked the orange dust from his fingers and motioned Carlos to help himself. "So, I checked with the brass. Cooperate with us on everything you know and we'll make the extortion charge go away. Of course, you're probably not welcome in Salt Lake City anymore, so we're prepared to move you, create a new identity, and allow you to lead a quiet life away from the limelight."

He pulled a map from his coat pocket. "Ever hear of Flatwoods, Kentucky? Not too far from West Virginia. Small town, not too hoity-toity. We can get you a job as a security guard. Mostly checking shopping malls, Walmarts, and Chuck E. Cheeses. Still, it's good, honest work."

Carlos bit into his sandwich as Sid continued. "No Wawas in Kentucky, Carlos. But there are 7-Elevens. At least you can get a Slurpee."

"What if they find me?"

"You'll have a contact. We get you out and send you somewhere else. Better if you just fit in and keep a low profile. Before you know it, you'll be a local." Sid laughed. "Maybe even develop a southern drawl."

CHAPTER 41

FBI Agent Mike Nelson read over the paperwork for Carlos Garcia. He was to be relocated, given a new identity, and advised to stay away from women who resemble Tina Turner.

New charges were filed against senior and middle management within the LDS. Miriam Connors, Bradshaw's former admin and confidant, decided to cooperate with the bureau and testify on current business practices in exchange for a reduced sentence. The church leadership planned to replace the fallen and tighten up oversight.

The picture of Carlos running shirtless and buckling his pants as Jasmine blew a kiss, became a meme within the FBI, the caption, "Check the goods before buying," advising caution in business transactions.

Mike left his apartment and drove to his favorite Starbucks, near the former Testimony Acres. He found a table, picked up his smoked shoulder bacon breakfast sandwich, blew on it in hopes of cooling it off, and took a big bite. He coughed as the roof of his mouth blistered from the molten bacon and cheese.

Donna Laurence, former barista, and now B-list actress, walked over from an adjacent table, and handed him a napkin. "You have to be careful. I used to work here. We nuke those things to make sure they're done all the way through."

He wiped his chin. "Thanks. The roof of my mouth feels like an abandoned nuclear site." He laughed. "Sort of like..."

Donna interrupted. "Testimony Acres?"

"Exactly." He studied the young woman. "I hope you weren't a disappointed buyer."

"No. My friend Louie told me about it one night."

"Louie, huh? Boyfriend?"

"Once, but mostly a casual acquaintance. I helped him with a management issue. I'm not sure I did much. They closed the place a few months later."

Mike took a swig of his juice. "I'm sure you were a big help."

Donna laughed, then pulled a chair and sat, examining her tablemate. "You look lonely. Wanna watch a movie in my apartment? Have you ever seen *Cool Hand Luke*?"

ABOUT THE AUTHOR

Tom Minder lives in New Jersey with his wife Paula. He is a member of the South Jersey Writers' Group and The Writers' Coffeehouse. His story *Burning for Rehoboth* won a judges award in the Beach Nights anthology from *Cat & Mouse Press*, 2016.

His prior novels include *The Long Harbor Testament* and *The House Always Wins*.

NOTE FROM THE AUTHOR

Word-of-mouth is crucial for any author to succeed. If you enjoyed *The Ferret*, please leave a review online—anywhere you are able. Even if it's just a sentence or two. It would make all the difference and would be very much appreciated.

Thanks!
Tom Minder

Thank you so much for reading one of Tom Minder's novels.
If you enjoyed the experience, please check out our
recommended title for your next great read!

The Long Harbor Testament by Tom Minder

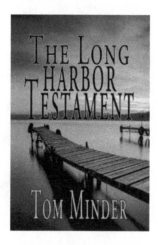

"A compelling and deftly crafted read from cover to cover"
-Midwest Book Review

View other Black Rose Writing titles at
www.blackrosewriting.com/books and use promo code
PRINT to receive a **20% discount** when purchasing.

9 781684 336593